THE WOLF

He was a Stewart, the son of a king of Scotland and born out of wedlock. He was married to a royal countess and he lived with a beautiful commoner. He was the legal representative of the National authority in territories north of the River Forth and he waged a bitter war on the Church in the Province of Moray and on its bishop Alexander Bur. He burned two towns, plundered an abbey and destroyed a great cathedral. He was excommunicated, condemned by his King, blackened by historians. Could anything good or new be said about such a man? Nothing, until chance uncovered the story of Philip Hogeston, soldier-priest, crusader and prisoner of the water-pit in the island castle of Lochindorb, the lair of the Wolf of Badenoch.

Published by

Librario Publishing Ltd

ISBN: 1-904440-18-5

(First published 2001 by Gopher Publishers UK. ISBN No: 90-76953-20-1)
This edition 2003

Copies can be ordered via the Internet
www.librario.com

or from:

Brough House, Milton Brodie, Kinloss
Moray IV36 2UA
Tel /Fax No 01343 850 617

Printed and bound by
DigiSource UK Ltd, Livingston

The Wolf

by

Charles Mackie

Librario

INTRODUCTION

The Winchester papers, or "The Lairdie's Papers"[1] as they are known here, were, literally, unearthed during the preliminary examination of Spynie Palace by the Department of the Environment. Centuries of weathering and quarrying have reduced to mounds of grassy rubble most of the high wall which surrounded the Palace. Yet the empty shell of the fortified tower-house, built by Bishop David Stewart for his own protection in 1461, heaves its squared bulk eighty feet above the turnip fields. North and east is marshland where there was a small harbour six hundred years ago, and less than a mile of water is all that remains of the Great Loch of Spynie. "Davy's Tower" sits astride the vitrified bones of an even older structure. This was the ancient Palace and Church of the Bishops of Moray from before the Cathedral at Elgin was built, until after its rape by the Wolf of Badenoch.

Sandy Dunbar, who inherited the old place from "The Lairdie", was pottering about in the dungeon beneath "Davy's Tower", used by his predecessor in his romantic years for purposes of his own. Sandy still cannot explain why he decided to turn over that particular flagstone, or how he even managed to shift it. He worked away for a long time with a crowbar and heavy hammer, until he got it moving, and there, in the snug, dry space below, was the box. He took it in his Land-Rover to Pitgaveny House where we carefully prized it open. The box was lead-lined, which explained its weight, and the scrolls and linen tablets were as dry as they had been when first laid inside.

Sandy was quick to guess at their antiquity.

"My God. Do you know what this is?"

I looked down at the Black Seal. "A Bishop's?" I asked.

"Bishop John Winchester's," said Sandy, "Bishop of Elgin Cathedral in the middle of the Fifteenth Century."

I called my wife and my secretary and spent the next four weeks at Pitgaveny. We got an expert up from Edinburgh and together sorted out the contents of the Bishop's chest. There were records of the building of the Cathedral in Elgin and the cost to Crown and Church of its damage by fire in 1390. There were documents that have thrown a grim light on the fate of the Comyn family in Scotland. But to me, the autobiography of Sir Philip Hogeston[2] was the prize find.

I have retold the story without I hope, altering it in any important way, except to translate the archaic idiom into understandable prose. Time has forced some compromise. For instance I find it impossible to describe the location of Lang or Long or Bishop's Steps, the extraordinary stone bridge that strode across the western narrows of the great loch of Spynie, without using present-day points of reference which were not there in Philip Hogeston's time. On the north side of the loch, the tidal marshes ended at Crosslots and the narrows were bridged by the Lang Steps, to beyond where Waterton Cottages are now. These two farms stand where bridle tracks twisted through reed and swan-grass on the night of the first ambush.

So also, syntax and vocabulary have had to be changed. Because I have studied his story very carefully, I know that the construction of Philip Hogeston's sentences, strange to us, was good colloquial writing, not too literary, but the normal stuff of everyday communication in 1439. The translation, of course, has meant using words Philip Hogeston could never have heard of, just as some of his vocabulary has vanished from present day use.

If we are agreed not to argue over small inconsistencies, then you can catch the mood of the writer and become spellbound as I was by his involvement in the burning of Elgin Cathedral by "The Wolf" in times not so very far removed from those of Merlin, Gramarye and the Lady of Shalott.

The Family Tree of **PHILIP HOGESTON**
born at Plewlands, Duffus, in the Earldom of Moray, A.D. 1370

1251 – King Alexander III of Scotland *m.* Princess Margaret *d.* of King Henry III of England

Princess Margaret *m.* King Eirik II of Norway

Princess Margaret (The Maid of Norway)
(In 1290, Princess Margaret, on her way to be Crowned Queen of Scotland, died in the Orkneys, Aged 7)

Queen Margaret died in 1282 and King Alexander III married Yolette de Dreux, a French heiress in 1285. He was killed in 1286 with no issue from this marriage.

Alastair MacDonald of The Isles *m.* Yolette de Dreux 1288

Matilde *m.* James Randolph

Bruce de Moray (Admiral) *m.* Caroline *d.* of the Earl of Mar

Euphemia *m.* James Hogeston of Plewlands

Philip *m.* Bridget de Dreux 1397

John   David   Catherine   Alastair   Jean

ONE

PLEWLANDS

March the First, 1437

A single event in my sixteenth year set the course my life has taken. If there had been no murder at the Bay of the Primroses I should not have met Bridget. May the ghosts of my dead friends forgive me such a thought. If I had not ambushed their murderers by the Long Steps my father would have had no cause to dispatch me to the Cathedral School in Elgin, as he said, "For the good of your soul and for my peace of mind." The last thing I wished for myself at the age of fifteen was to become a priest. I would not then have been in the Cathedral that violent night of the seventeenth of June or have been carried like a gralloched stag to a wolf's lair at Lochindorb.

On the brief occasions that my father was at home he was full of talk about the warring feuds of the border country. He was a strong soldierly man who spent most of his life, and nearly all his fortune, fighting the Sassenach. He would tell us of the siege of Roxburgh, its relief and its recapture, and of the terrible burning of Edinburgh by the English. My boyhood escapades were coloured by these war stories and we "killed" the English from the caves of Duffus to the rocks of Birnie.

My bosom friend and rival in those days was a St. Kilda lad who had come to live in Hopeman with his auntie when his father was drowned guga hunting on the sheer cliffs of that faraway island. His mother had quickly taken another mate. He was a natural bragger, but I suspected with plenty to brag about. His story of the journey from St. Kilda to Stornoway and from there through the Pentland Firth to Hopeman in a tiny fishing vessel, was hair-raising enough to be strictly true. His greatest asset was his long, slender, muscular toes, a hereditary feature of those dwelling on that ancient rock sprung from the bowels of the Northern sea. Their livelihood depended on the harvest of the gugas, the immature nestlings of the solan geese, who in their thousands laid their eggs on the high ledges of the sea precipices. It was said they travelled the length of the world to nest at St. Kilda, wintering in the surf of Africa. Eric Bigfeet and I became friends when I got stuck on Groff Hochs, a massive pile of rock along the coast from Hopeman, where the falcons nested. I was on a ledge which ended in an overhang with nothing below but foaming surf. Eric was fishing offshore in his uncle's little coracle, bobbing up and down in the waves and hauling in the whiting and haddock from the sandy seabed. He saw me but paid little notice, until in desperation I yelled and yelled for help. The tide was coming in and already the sea thundered in white spume between the thick sandstone legs, which gave the rock its name. At that time I could not swim and it would be twelve hours later, three in the morning, before I ever got ashore, even if I did succeed in escaping from this damned ledge.

Eric came close in and hurled himself from the little flat boat on to the lowest of the ledges beneath me. He knew the waves would wash the boat ashore and that the jagged rock would never harm the frail looking, light skin craft. He climbed to me quickly, long strong toes gripping crevices and tiny ledges as he ran almost vertically up the cliff.

"Now you damn fool son of a pig," he shouted at me. "Get your fat arse off that ledge and on to my shoulders."

My cowardice evaporated at these calculated insults and rage propelled me into the intricate contortions necessary to place my "fat arse" on Eric's back. Inch by inch, breaking my fingernails, and relying on Eric's strong toes and superb balance, I was rescued from the ledge. We dropped the final ten feet into the surf and slithered our way to the shingle beneath the cliffs. Eric's first remark was "Hey Oggie, you'll have to learn to swim."

A week later, we had a ride together, which I shall never forget. We rode from Plewlands towards the Castle and crossed the neck of the Loch by the Lang Steps. We took the woodland path over Cuttieshillock, past the farms of Mosstowie and Miltonduff and up the valley of the River Lossie to the Buinach. We were making for the moors that stretched from the Lossie to the Spey to hunt for hill gull's eggs. These, laid by gulls feeding on farmland, are very good to eat and taste just like plovers' eggs. We found the nesting places away beyond the Latterach Burn, high on the lonely moors, and had returned to the valley of the Shougle. Before joining the River Lossie, this little burn rushes headlong in precipitous plungings and gurglings all the way down a steep gorge, through deep rocky pools and dripping cliffs.

We left our horses free to forage and slipped through the birch woods to explore. Brambles trailed low by the banks and the stream sped into a narrow throat. We had been there often before but never in such a flood. Wet to the skin and slimy with green mud, we came to the middle pool, a broad, deep loch of a place in low water but now a seething cauldron of bubbles, spray and foam. The burn from above splashed into the middle of this and behind the fall was a cave quite hidden by the curtain of water. Leaping through the torrent we landed on moss. It was beautiful to look back at the light through the tumbling waterfall, and the older boys, to test their courage as well as to show off to the younger ones, would dive outwards through the screen into the invisible deep pool beyond. But today we were not alone in this cave. We had scarcely got our breath back when our blood froze and the hairs on the napes of our necks bristled with primitive fear. There was a sharp, feline stench and the unmistakable harsh hiss of a wildcat. We flattened ourselves against the walls. I was the bigger and struck my head a crack on the roof. The hiss continued, and, as our eyes grew accustomed to the dark, we could make out the baleful, unflickering eyes of the beast, crouched near the back wall and the tiny sparks of yellow that were eyes of her kits. There is no animal in all Scotland, stag, wolf, fox, bear, otter or boar, quite so fearsome as the full-grown mother wildcat protecting her young. She can, in an instant, become a thunder ball of scratching, spitting, biting fury, which no boy of fifteen would dare to face.

Through gritted teeth Eric whispered, "I'm getting out of here. Follow me and I'll look after you in the water," and with one leap he vanished through the roaring fall. I was alone, very, very, much alone. To my left, within touching distance almost, crouched an animal the size of a large terrier, all tooth and claw and hate and ready to launch herself at my face. To my right, a leap into nothingness and a death by drowning in a bottomless pool. I had again to trust my friend Eric and hope that he was there to seize me as I plummeted into the water. I took a deep breath and leapt through the thundering white screen. It pelted down on me for an instant.

"Hold your nose," shrieked Eric. I hit the water and splashed into its bubbly blackness, then bobbed to the surface struggling for very life. Perceptibly the thunder of the fall grew less. I felt myself in the gentle grip of the burn and, oh, miracle, I was floating. In a vigorous dog's paddle I projected myself with the help of the current towards the bank. My fears vanished. I was swimming! A moment or two later I hoisted myself on the rocks at the far side having swum twenty yards and feeling proud of myself. But where was Eric?

"Here, you bloody fool," he shouted down to me. When he jumped out through the fall he had struck the branch of a birch tree, which hung over the water. This had caught on his belt and there he was suspended like a lamb's carcass on a butcher's hook. The paradox of the situation suddenly struck me and I roared and yelled with laughter.

"Get me down, you glayked gyte," he stuttered. I swung on the branch and we both fell into the water where we splashed about like young otters and, with bravado that follows fear, threw stones up into the cave.

Some years later I had to swim for my life to escape from another wild animal, not a wild cat but a wolf – The Wolf of Badenoch.

Two

When we were not slaughtering the English or slaying the Vikings – the legends of Haakon the Bold and Eric the Red are real enough to us who live on the coast of the Moray Firth – we were exploring the labyrinth of caves in the sandstone cliffs between Causea and Hopeman. There were seven other boys who shared the adventures of my sixteenth year. Eric Bigfeet was my particular crony. The Bews twins, "Chucker" and "Blether", were born in Orkney on a croft at Orphir overlooking the Scapa Flow. Chucker could throw a stone with accuracy fifty yards, a performance that was to cost him his life, and Blether could not hold his tongue for longer than it took to ask his name. The crop disaster in the stormy summer of 1380 had forced this family to move to the mainland and they farmed a croft at Stotfield to the West of Lossiemouth. The four of us were often joined by the Chisholm boys from the Castle when they could free themselves from their mother's apron strings. Two serving lads from the Castle hung round hopefully. One of them, "Cleeky", an expert at "cleeking", or hooking out partan crabs from the rocks, was prepared to "borrow" his father's boat as the price of joining us. The other, "The Gomeril", who could assume a deceptive idiot expression, sometimes volunteered as our scapegoat.

Lessons held us to the schoolroom at the Castle in the mornings, but in the afternoons of Spring and Summer we were free to act out the dreams of boyhood in the woods or down at the Loch or among the sea cliffs. There was one bay which we knew as "The Bay of the Primroses" because in June its steep green slopes are a mass of yellow stars. Its square sandy beach lies between forbidding cliffs, the home of hundreds of seabirds. Above this bay there are some heaps of rust-brown rubble we called "War Towers" which may have been Pict or Christian outposts during the savage centuries of survival against the Vikings. From there, on a midsummer evening, the hills of Caithness and Sutherland float on a pellucid sea while the sun dips behind the shoulder of Ben Wyvis and rises three hours later above the Paps of Morven.

During that hot June we explored every crag, every pool and every cave in the miles of cliff and sea-worn sandstone between the beach at Causea and the village of Hopeman. It was inevitable I suppose that seven inquisitive boys should sooner or later stumble upon the secret of this ancient shore. East of the Bay of the Primroses, behind a high pile of fallen rocks cloaked in seapinks and nettles, we dug away sand from the base of the cliff and found the entrance to a long narrow cave. Its slimy floor dried into dark sand marked only by the tiny spoors of rodents. We lit some drift-wood and the flames flickered on the yellow stone of a cavern with walls blackened in part by the soot of ancient fires. One of the Chisholm boys found drawings on the rock and we looked in amazement at pictures of shaggy bulls, wolves, and animals we had never seen.

"Look at the smoke," said Eric, and we watched the pale-blue haze coil and swirl into the darkness beyond our circle of light. We followed it and found the steps, chiselled out of the sandstone by the tread of many feet. We took flaming brands from the fire and climbed upwards. The steps ended in a fall of rubble.

"We must be near the top," said the Gomeril. "There's dried peat amongst these stanes." We dug away at the dirt, coughing as the smoke from below swirled past us.

"Yer right," said Eric. "The fug's gaain' somewhere."

A chink of light appeared and a fall of earth nearly knocked us off the steps. Blether Bews squeezed through the gap and we heard a muffled stream of oaths when he hauled himself clear and into a dense clump of gorse. We scrambled out into the bramble and whin of the moor not fifty yards from Plewlands. The cave became our meeting place, our den. We called it the Cave of the Picts although I suspect now that the men who carved the steps and decorated the walls with their drawings had lived long before the painted men fought with the Roman legions at Mons Graupius.[3]

The adventure which had most impact on the course of my life happened after a week of storm at the time of the September Equinox. My sister and I were awakened at dawn by shouts, the sound of running feet and the voice of Sime the smith booming above the hubbub.

"Get Lady Eupheme. Aye, wake her ye daft quine. She will tell us what to do." We were down in a trice.

"What is it Sime?" I asked. Sime, a puzzled look on his bearded face, extended an arm towards me and opened his large fist.

In the palm of his hand was a green enamelled brooch with an engraved head in the middle flanked by a row buck and a swan.

"Where did you get it," I asked.

"Here, young master," said the smith, and, like a conjurer, he plucked a doll-like figure from behind his legs. The man was small and clad in tatters. He had flaxen hair matted by sea salt and a gold ring glinted on his right ear. My mother spoke behind us.

"Who is he Sime, and where is he from?"

"That, I don't know my lady," said Sime. "John the Greek found him in the gardens. But he is either too full of fear or too empty-headed to speak to us." My mother looked at the man, then slowly, in French, she talked to him.

"Are you a matelot?" she asked. Spoken to kindly and in a tongue he could understand, the sailor shrugged himself free from Sime's grip and stammered out his story. His ship, the Monica, thirteen days out of Copenhagen and bound for Aberdeen had run before the gale into the Moray Firth. In the night, lost and dismasted, she struck on the dreaded Halliman Skerries and, lifted free by wave and storm, was driven sinking to the shore. She beached, in a welter of white water, in the Bay of the Primroses.

"Are there any men still aboard her?" asked Lady Eupheme.

"There might be," replied the sailor, but his eyes told us he would be surprised if they were alive.

"Who gave you this?" She took the green brooch from Sime.

"One of the passengers, a holy man, a very brave man who called on God to stop the storm – but how could God hear in such a tempest."

"Send the brooch at once to Bishop Bur," commanded my mother. "Every man must go to the cliff top. There may be lives to save."

We found the wreck and my sister Elsie and I, searching the caves behind the heaps of seadrift and shingle, came upon a shivering group of men lying exhausted on the sand. They included the Captain of the Monica who wept as he watched the death-throes of his ship. His name was Thor Rifsun and, when they were warm and dry at Plewlands, those of his crew and passengers who survived told us how he had struggled to hold his vessel in the teeth of a gale he knew was too strong for him or any man.

Back at Plewlands we met the first of the many folk who came from Elgin that day and in the days to follow, to watch the break up of the wreck and to gather what they could of the flotsam on the shore. And by the first ferry from Spynie came two Black Friars. They asked to speak with Sir James Hogeston and saw me instead, and my mother. They told us they were emissaries from Bishop Bur sent with haste to enlist our help in a secret and most important matter. They did not tell us immediately the nature of this but questioned us about the shipwreck and about the survivors. These, they insisted on seeing, the injured as well as the fit, and asked them to describe in minutest detail the last moments of the stricken ship. They questioned Thor Rifsun about his passengers and about their baggage. I was consumed with curiosity as to what these crow-like sinister men were seeking.

"What was that all about?" I asked as soon as we were back in my father's room. The cowelled men exchanged glances. The one who had been most persistent in his interrogation spoke, but so quietly and from the concealment of his cowl that I had to strain my ears to catch his words.

"Madame et Monsieur, you are witnesses to a most unfortunate occurrence. Many men have been lost and a king's ransom lies at the bottom of the sea. The ship, the Monica, carried Bishop Pius, the emissary of his holiness the Pope. This we know, for this brooch belonged to him. Bishop Pius was to have represented the Mother Church at the consecration of the Chapel of St. Brinuth in Elgin Cathedral. We are certain he was the one who called in vain on God to calm the storm. He is dead. God rest his soul in peace. He bore with him from Avignon a treasure whose loss is more to be regretted than the death of Ten Bishops. He was responsible for delivering a gift from King Robert to Bishop Bur, a gift blessed by the Pope's holy hand." He paused. His eyes glittered from the shadow of his hood.

"Two solid, carved, golden candlesticks, five feet tall, and a golden chalice three spans wide. They must be found." His voice had become a hoarse whisper and small flecks of white spit formed on his lips. "Each wave must be watched, every rock pool searched until God delivers up His treasure."

My feelings at that moment were conflicting. The golden ornaments, worth a prince's ransom, kindled a blaze of excitement. Yet this cold insistence on their recovery linked to the callous dismissal of the death of Bishop Pius and others as a matter of little consequence set my skin prickling with faint horror. I looked again at these sombre creatures, listened to the menace of cruel intensity in their voices, and shuddered. They were the merciless inquisitors of a God who had exchanged pity for cupidity. I believe that was the moment when for the first time I doubted the righteousness of the Church; the moment when heresy took seed.

There were no lessons for the next week because from dawn to dusk we were at the Bay of the Primroses. A guard was mounted. Men and women, boys and girls searched the beach and the rocks, and all day long the Black Friars paced the cliff-path, robes spread by the breeze like bats-wings. A week after the shipwreck we were picking over the debris left by the tides of the equinox in a small cliff-bound bay half a mile to the West. The sea was calm and a long swell beat on the shore.

"Let's look in the sea-cave," suggested someone, and six naked bodies splashed their way to the cave entrance. This was a hole in the cliff visible above the waves only at full ebb. Now, it was four feet under sea. One by one we duck-dived and six bottoms flashed and vanished like the white breasts of guillemots. We swam through the hole and bobbed up gasping and whooping inside a cave. There was a clatter and swoosh of invisible wings as a roosting of doves fled like arrows to the exit high above. The cave was lit from below. Emerald light, reflected up from the sandy floor of the bay outside, illuminated rock which dripped with seaweed the colour of ox-blood.

"Hey lads! What's that down there?" The Blether, who had climbed on to a rock, dived deep to the sea-bed. He came struggling to the surface yelling, "Help me for Cris-sake. I've found the Pope's bloody treasure!" Five pairs of hands grabbed at Bew's find.

"Ye damn fools. Now ye've dropped it. Stop shoving. Phil, come down with me and give a hand." I knew what I held as soon as I touched it. It was the Bishop's Chalice, a bowl of gold two feet in diameter. It took us some time to swim the Chalice out of the cave and back to the shore for the tide was ebbing and pulled against us. Then came our second piece of luck.

"Look," cried Chucker, "A candlestick." Wedged in a rock crevice where the sea foamed was a carved golden candlestick so heavy that we had a job freeing it. Then Chucker spotted the other one, rolling slowly under the sea beyond the wave burst. Our tiny coracles sank with the added weight so we hid the treasure in a heap of bird-dung and rowed for home. The news we brought sparked off a flurry of activity. The two Friars insisted, although it was now late in the day, that the treasure must be taken back to their safe-keeping. A boat was made ready and the Bews twins, who had found the ornaments, joined the men as guides, while the Gomeril was dispatched on horseback to break the good news to Bishop Bur. He chose to ride by the Lang Steps rather than take the slower route by ferry across the Loch of Spynie.

"Dinna lose the stuff Sime afore I come back," he called in jest to the boats' leader. Not only was the treasure lost but the Gomeril never came back. Too late to warn us of disaster ahead, his body was found near the Southern end of the Long Steps. His skull had been smashed in. The message to Bishop Bur had vanished.

At the coming of dusk a cold seaward breeze sprang up and we found a sheltered place in the lee of the cliff top. There is a ledge just below the crest, and the Chisholm boys, Eric and I snuggled down there to wait the boat's return. The warm September day was over. A hazy sun prepared to set behind the mountains of Sutherland and the bay took on the colour of a pigeon's breast. Round the headland came the boat. At that moment a low voice spoke behind and above us and something in the speaker's tone made us flatten ourselves against the cliff and hold our breaths.

"There she is, and the gold will be ashore in ten minutes. Keep your horses below the skyline and ride to the track at the West of the Bay. The plan will succeed if we surprise them. They must think we come from Bishop Bur so act like couriers. Be bold but courteous. I shall do the talking. Keep your weapons hidden and with luck we shall not need to show them. Alexander, your job is to get to the two friars and divert their attention while we load up the saddlebags. They must not be allowed to interfere, or killing will become necessary." There was a soft flurry of hooves on the moor behind us, then silence.

"Guid's sake, what di ye mak o' thon?" Answering his own question, Eric continued "Bishop's men! – Bloody robbers mair like! We'll hae tae stop them."

"How?" I asked.

"If we use the short cut we will be on the beach before them." We jumped down to the sand just as the boat grounded on the shingle.

"Listen." There was the telltale clatter of loose stones as the horses reached the shore.

"Look out," I shrieked. "You are going to be robbed." The men in the boat heard us, and so did the horsemen. Someone cursed loudly and hooves beat urgently on the soft machair above the sands. The boat was bow's-out of the sea but with speed the crew might have pushed her back into the waves and rowed to safety. They were no cowards these men of ours. With a yell they leaped ashore. I saw Sime hurl himself at the leading horseman and horse and man crashed to the ground. I saw "Chucker" Bews heaving pebbles as fast as he could pick them up. He had the strongest throw of all of us and a shouted curse indicated that his aim had been good. Then it happened. To my horror I saw the flash of steel. Wee Bews had been reaching down for another stone when suddenly a round object, which could only be his head, rolled towards the sea and two black spouts poured from his neck. The scene had developed into bloody nightmare. Weeping with fear and rage the Chisholms, Eric and I took to our heels and ran for the Cave of the Picts and in minutes reached the small exit on the moor. Eric vomited into a whin-bush.

I was sixteen years old. I had looked on the bloated corpses of men whom I had known, thrown up by the sea; men made unrecognisable by what the sea had done to them. I had sneaked into a house to discover what a dead man looked like who had died from drink. But the murder of poor little Bews, before my eyes on the beach at the Bay of the Primroses, was the most frightening thing that had ever happened to me. By the time we had reached the stables at Plewlands, I had gained control of my fear and was ashamed of my cowardice. Anger took possession of me, anger at myself and at the raiders. I turned on my companions. "Come on Eric, and you Chisholms. There's only one way off the island to the mainland that the murderers can take. We can catch them at the Lang Steps. Get on your horses." The Bishop's or the Lang Steps lie across the narrow part of the Loch, South-east from the Castle of Duffus and are of hewn blocks set five feet apart paved with flagstones. From the oak forest the ground slopes gradually towards these Steps and a pathway continues the final half mile across the salt marshes. We boys knew every island of the Loch, almost every waterhen's nest along its verge, and in darkness we could pick our way from reed clump to reed clump. There was a fowler's island some twenty yards from the last step and to this we cantered, after collecting our Welsh longbows. Mine had been given to me by my father for my fifteenth birthday. It had been copied at the Castle by the armourer and both the twins and Eric had similar weapons. They were fearsome things for young boys to use but, with practice, we developed a knack of bending them which produced very satisfactory results up to about sixty yards. But this was different. Hares, partridges and even wild geese we had shot at and hit, but never men.

It was dark when we reined our horses at the salt flats, slapped their haunches and set them cantering back towards Plewlands. We lay on Fowler's Island fifteen minutes before we felt, rather than heard, the sound of galloping horses, and there they were, reining in to pick their way along the narrow path towards the Steps with the tide rising steadily. We waited until they were almost on us and then fired our first flight. The foremost rider fell sideways. He was held by the stirrups and his mount floundered into the thick marshy water, trailing him by the boots. There was a roar of rage from the middle of the group. "Get on the steps, we are ambushed." Their confusion was such that our second flight of arrows missed completely. I was sighting my third arrow on the head of a man who had given the command when he turned to face directly towards me. In the moonlight I saw a bushy beard, black eyebrows, and a grimace of sheer fury as the arrow sped on its way. That baleful glance unsighted me for there was a thud and a bitten off shout of pain. The man had been hit but I had missed his face. Then the riders reached the Steps. We sent a volley after them but by now they were out of range and taking off like the wind along the causeway. They took a risk at speed on that narrow flagstone bridge, with the sea flowing in beneath them. We yelled with triumph and cut the dead man from his floundering horse. We were avenged.

Little Bews was avenged and the Gomeril too, though we did not know then that he was dead.

The bearded horseman's face rooted itself in my memory. Four years later, in captivity, I was to curse my poor aim with all my soul and wish my shot had flighted straight to one of these blazing eyes.

Three

This last disastrous adventure could not be overlooked even by my most tolerant of mothers and a message was sent urgently seeking my father's return. When he arrived some three weeks later he cross-examined me about my part in the affair at the Bay of the Primroses. He asked me to tell him about the robbers and, in particular, about the man I had shot at and winged.

"Well I'll be damned," he swore softly, but did not tell me who it was he had recognised from my description. Life at Plewlands was suddenly serious. There was a visit from the Bishop of Moray, Alexander Bur. I was warned to be clean and at hand if his Eminence condescended to see me. This he did and I was confronted by a different pair of baleful eyes. His were pale and set on a white pasty complexion in a face that resembled the features of the inscrutable sphinx.

"Boy," a resonant voice boomed with surprising vigour from a scrawny neck.

"Boy, do you wish to join the Church of God?" I had expected this question. After a great deal of parental persuasion I had succumbed to this unattractive idea. I answered in truth that I could not admit to wishing to join the Church. I had been persuaded that it was the only course open to me. The Bishop fell silent and scrutinised me through those pale fish eyes of his.

"Scarcely an enthusiastic supplication, but we shall endeavour to make something of this unlikely material." What he said next surprised me, coming from a Bishop.

"I hear you think you are a passable bowman. You must improve your aim."

My youthful days of freedom were over. Gone were the blue days, the green days, the brown days of a boy's crowded life. The cage of manhood was about to snap shut. My education hitherto had been by tutors, young men of some learning who had been hired to instruct us in Euclid, French and Latin. The Chisholm boys and girls from the Castle, my sisters Elsie and Mary, Eric and the Bews twins were my companions. I suspect that the latter were added to the group because my parents considered their freedom to be an unendurable temptation to me. We acquired some formal learning. We had one good tutor, a young novice from Pluscarden Abbey, who had studied physic in the University of Montpellier. He had the biggest feet I had ever seen, an infectious laugh and jagged teeth. They were broken, he told us, defending the Faith in an alehouse in Paris.

The murder at Primrose Bay ended this and I was banished to the Cathedral School to brush up my Latin before taking passage for Paris and the Scots College. These days are supposed to be the happiest of our lives and I suppose my three years in Paris were happy enough. I met, wooed and made love to a rare variety of girls, Hungarian, French, Scots, Danish, Turkish, Spanish and Arab. Paris was the centre of all the world and sooner or later everyone met on the banks of the Seine or in Notre-Dame Cathedral. I lived on a farm. In the summer I worked from four in the morning until eight and then again from six in the evening to ten. The harvest had to be fitted in to allow us to attend classes, and in the winter the classes were fitted around our other commitments and amusements. The system worked quite well for it was understood by our professors and produced the credits at the end of term which kept our fathers happy. I pursued with enthusiasm my hobby of weaponry and graduated with paper trophies in Latin, French and theology and with a practical understanding and expertise in wrestling, swordsmanship and archery. My religious instruction was a mixed study of classical dogma and the New Thought. We were in the era of pope and anti-pope and although Scotland, Spain and France adhered to the Pope in Avignon there was a great split in

Christendom. Questions were being whispered in salons, bistros and in student lodgings which even ten years before would have been unthinkable. Had adoration become idolatory? Had the message of Christ been lost in all the pomp, pageantry and rich trappings of the established Church? Had corruption defaced religious practice? France was at the height of her power. The English possessions had been wrested from them and in the decadence which followed the ravages of war all sorts of heresies sprouted like wild vetch in a field of wheat.

In 1388 I was summoned home. My father had been slain on the field at Otterburn, in that dreadful moonlight battle, and my mother called me back. My ecclesiastic studies were incomplete, and out of deference to my father's wish, I attached myself once more to Bishop Bur and the "Sang" School to continue my pursuit of grace. But I was restless. I had lost something in Paris – or had I gained something else? My old complacency had been dented and I had begun to doubt the rightness of the right. Certain sacred cows had been revealed as scraggy old beasts, and there had been nothing in the cynical, satirical atmosphere of student Paris to fill the void left by the fallen idols. I was glad to return to my clean northern air, to scent again the myrtle of the wide moors and taste the blaeberries under the alder trees. My heart lifted to the sight of snow on the hills of Caithness and on the Sutherland of the Vikings. Morven reared her cone in the winter sky, sunsets were brighter than they had ever been while as always the Loch of Spynie raised its shining face to the heavens and welcomed its skeins of geese and squadrons of swans.

And so in the year 1390 I had celebrated my twentieth birthday, was Laird of Plewlands and novice to the Bishop of Moray in the Cathedral of Elgin, known to all men as the Lantern of the North. The months I spent within the cloisters of this beautiful place were distressing months for Bishop Bur and his canons and monks. I was a disrupting influence in their midst, having a head full of dangerous new ideas, hot from France. I had found it easy to despise the gawdy glitter of pomp and wealth while I lived the life of a poor scholar in

Paris. I had succumbed, of course, to that usual student malaise of impatience and impertinence which condemned all institutions of the day and brooked no compromise with the past.

I have found poverty in all the great towns that I have visited. But in Paris, most of all, the poor were there in their thousands and in their rags, jostling, begging, fighting for scarce scraps of food and dying filthy in the gutters. The contrast with the powdered, scented ladies of the court and their fine consorts in rich leathers and linens, with their plumed hats and jewelled swords, assaulted the senses like the stench of sewage in the Seine after a downpour. Alongside the stark horrors of the destitute were the rich ornaments, the gold and the gawdy vestments of the Church.

Here, a whole world away from that teeming city life, my young and unforgiving eyes were picking out these identical symptoms of decadence and indulgence that I had ranted about in the bistros of Montmartre. I noted the mutual lack of affection between the common folk in Elgin and the community of the Cathedral. The pitiful condition of the unfortunates in the leper colony outside the East Gate was known, but disregarded by all save a very few. Mark you, I was not of the few. My criticism did not engender my own involvement for although I rather fancied myself as the reforming zealot who would change all this, I did not relish soiling my hands in the process. I was thoroughly disliked. I pried into every dubious undertaking and scented out all mysterious or suspicious happenings. Thus I stumbled on the shame of the Urquhart Priory and on the jealousies which existed between the Bishop and the Benedictines of Pluscarden. Yet despite my discovery of unchristian conduct meted out to each other by this brotherhood of God, and despite the certainty of longstanding immoral practices, deep within me I was absolutely convinced of the truths of the Christian gospel and of the need of these pure ethics in the times we live in. These conflicting images preoccupied me, for it remained a paradox and a puzzle unsolved that in surroundings of such serene and noble beauty created by men whose minds must have been touched by God, there should remain this rottenness in the hearts of others. So I prayed for the souls of all but myself, for my own had not begun to exist.

As often as I could I returned to Plewlands. The Loch of Spynie abounded with wild fowl. Coot and waterhen were there by the thousand. Mallard duck nested in the reeds. Swans sailed like fighting ships on its surface and fashioned their huge island nests among the rushes. Terns screamed over the shingle beds to the East and hundreds of black-headed gulls built a noisy busy colony in the marshes to the South of the Bishop's palace. Later in the year migrating birds filled the air with the sound of their wings, the teal, the golden eye, and the greylag geese from the far north. In the pine trees between the Loch and the River Lossie there was a heronry and at all seasons, if you looked very carefully, you could glimpse the shape of these silent, motionless fishers, standing knee deep in the mud, their beaks poised for the unwary fish or frog.

I think my companions at the Cathedral put up with my long pious face and disapproving eyes because of the good things I took back to them from my hours of freedom. My saddlebags would be heavy with wild duck taken in the traps set by Matthew the Fowler or there would be a brace of swans torn from the sky by my peregrine, Kitty. During the nesting season some dozens of black-headed gulls' eggs found their way, hard-boiled, to the tables of the Maisondieu.

Four

During the first six months of that fateful year 1390, one man dominated out thoughts and our conversation. He was Alexander Stewart, King's son, Justiciar of Scotland North of the Forth, Earl of Buchan and Ross and Lord of Badenoch. For years our Bishop, Alexander Bur, had ridden a collision course with this man, and all of us in the Cathedral Community now knew that explosion could not long be avoided. The Bishop's temporal power extended into the wild hill country of Badenoch, bounded in the South by the Cairngorms and in the North by the valley of the Findhorn. In the heart of this waste of moor and mountain lay Lochindorb, a wind-swept expanse of water surrounding an island castle, the home of the Lord of Badenoch. The extension of the Bishop's power into territory, which, of all his possessions, Alexander Stewart considered his closest personal domain, rankled and became the object of legal wrangling which lasted ten years and ended in ravage by fire.

The first confrontation between these two men had been staged by the Earl who told the Bishop to renounce his claim to the Church lands in Badenoch. Bishop Bur resisted this demand. As justiciar – the King's legal representative – Stewart summoned Bur to appear before his court at the Standing Stones of Easter Kingussie. There, not unexpectedly, the Bishop's claim to the Badenoch lands was rejected. Bishop Bur read the writing on the wall. Out of this small rebuff he foresaw the gradual assimilation of his rich territories by this predatory prince. More important still was the effect of this decision on the Church which, growing in power and influence, aimed at the domination of temporal as well as spiritual affairs in Scotland that she had achieved elsewhere, notably in France.

At Ruthven in Badenoch a year or two later, these two powerful, ambitious men met again. Since their first confrontation Bishop Bur had been active. One would have thought the entire Faith was at stake, so assiduously had he prepared for this moment. Gathered on his side at the Justiciar's Court in Ruthven Castle was the power and the strength of the Church. Like all young men since at the Cathedral School, I was obliged to memorise the names of the churchmen present, and the list sounded like a Roll Call of Archangels! Faced with this adamant, glittering array of the powerful men of the Mother Church both in Scotland and from France, and placed under duress by a thinly veiled ecclesiastical threat, Alexander Stewart saw that he had met his match and before the assembled Court, he burnt his papers of proof.

The history of these events was well known to all of us at the Cathedral for Bishop Bur had not been slow to proclaim his victory. The clangour of Church bells announced it throughout the Province. Masses were held in his honour. He arranged processions to the furthermost Churches in Badenoch – processions scarcely to be distinguished from armed sorties, so strong was his bodyguard and so flamboyant his banners. In 1390 matters were made even worse between the Bishop and the Lord of Badenoch by the intervention of Stewart's brother now King Robert the Third. For his own reasons, Stewart had deserted his lawful wife Euphemia Countess of Ross whom he had married purely for his own aggrandizement. He lived now in Lochindorb with his mistress, Mariota Athyn, the mother of all his children. The King, prompted by the Bishop, could do no other than support Bur's uncompromising defence of the deserted Euphemia and commanded his headstrong brother to abandon his mistress.

We expected strong rhetoric from our Bishop on this subject and we were not disappointed. Once a week he addressed his budding clerics in the Church of the Maisondieu. We enjoyed these tirades for we then heard "Old Sticky-Bur" at his vituperative best. He knew that he was addressing a "bunch of young heretics" and was at pains to defend the "tried and proved" methods of the Church. A word he was fond of using was "reprobate" – "unworthy of salvation". Any of us boys who implied even the mildest criticism of the establishment was instantly, by Sticky-Bur's definition and epithet "A fornicating reprobate". We were accustomed then to hearing this intriguing phrase hurled at our, sometimes, deserving selves. But when, in a torrent of rage, he applied to the Lord of Badenoch this choice description, we were quite convulsed by almost uncontrollable joy. The Arch-enemy of the Provincial Church had suddenly been compared with our unworthy persons – a pack of unruly, dissenting and oft-time fornicating novices. The label stuck. We loved it and soon it was a catch-phrase in Elgin. Had the Earl heard it he might have enjoyed it too, and who knows, the Cathedral might never have been burnt! But, alas, he did not, and his reply, addressed to his adversary and tormentor, Bishop Bur, was brief and uncompromising. It contained a statement of intent: should the Bishop not surrender to him his possessions in Badenoch and in Moray, he must suffer the direct consequence. His message is said to have ended "nemo me impune lacessit" – no one meddles in my affairs with impunity.

Hard on this warning in May, came the burning of Forres. To hear the Forres folk talk you would be forgiven for thinking the whole town was destroyed. It was the Bishop's properties that the Lord of Badenoch fired; the Archdeacon's place was burnt to the ground, the Church was partly destroyed and houses close by suffered damage. The Bishop retaliated with the dreadful Ban of Excommunication. The fateful words we knew by heart as we young fellows were expected to. "The Holy Church shall cut thee off like a rotten and diseased branch to fall headlong into The Pit where eternal fire shall consume thee." It followed that every man's hand was set against him and that his slaying would rejoice the Church. None dared. That fearful curse had but one dire result, Alexander Stewart became thereafter "The Wolf of Badenoch", a name he encouraged. His descent upon Forres from his stronghold in Lochindorb was described by Bishop Bur as "An horrid act of sacrilege and vandalism" and this devil-man was soon pictured in the public eye as possessing gigantic strength. We heard stories of his enormous black horse with eyes that flashed fire, teeth which champed on children and mothers brought their families scurrying indoors with the threat "The Wolf'll get ye".

To us of the Church, his assaults on the lands and buildings and purse and people of the Bishopric were the unprovoked and deliberate acts of the anti-Christ. But if the Bishop had thought to deter the Wolf by the fearful curse of excommunication, we younger churchmen were not so convinced. Four of us discussed it among ourselves and decided that should this demon descend on Elgin we were not prepared to submit without a fight. We knew that to wield a sword in anger was totally against the rules of the Church, as it was against the rules of the Maisondieu to keep any form of offensive weapon, but we managed to smuggle in and to hide a fair armoury under the flooring in our cells. So, when it happened on a cold June evening thick with haar, we were not caught unprepared. The great bells of the Cathedral awakened us with their clamour. The shouts and screams of frightened families running from the manses to the sanctuary got us out of our beds with a rush and we heard the cry – "The Wolf, the Wolf". We raced to arm, uncovered our swords and round shields, tied our helmets under our chins and ran towards the burning manses. Flames were already leaping from the windows as these houses, largely made of wood, went up in smoke. There was running and shouting as the wild hill-men capered and whooped and threw their resin torches on the roofs and anywhere that would burn.

Several closes lead from the college grounds to the Cathedral. We took a close each and, in the pale misty light, hacked and stabbed at the Highlanders with their flaming brands as they rushed from their destruction of the manses towards the Cathedral. For a few minutes the appearance of armed resistance astonished the attackers. We knew that by trial and error they would soon find the mouths of the unguarded closes and we were ready for them when they came at us from our rear. Three of us fought our way to the Cathedral. Rory the Skye man failed to join us. When we reached the iron-bound doors they were barred tight as we had half expected, and the horde, attracted by the clash of swords, swooped down upon us. Donald, wounded and bleeding, was out of the fight. Hamish shouted "Good luck, Phil," and started to cut his way like a war chariot into the leaping press of men. From near by came a commanding shout. In an instant the battle ceased, our attackers cowered back, and, for a moment, I thought we had won. My arm was tired. My targe in shreds but my sword was still up and I yelled, "Fight on you carrion or I'll cut you to chicken feed."

There came another command in the Old Tongue and a scuffle of feet. Above me I heard a rushing sound and, before I knew what was happening, a net fell on me and I was spread-eagled, face down on the cobblestones, with a dozen hands on my throat and arms. The leader spoke again. I was trussed up like a pullet for the pot and slung across a horse's back.

At that very moment the first of the firebrands soared into the sky to crash through the stone tracery of the western window. Further showers of flaming arrows arched up on the parapets and higher yet into the guttering of the roof. The inferno of the blazing manses showered swarms of busy sparks, drifted thick wood smoke towards us, and crackled its message of doom to the threatened building. Each burst of new flame on the Cathedral's roof was greeted by a cheer of triumph from the attackers – cheers which competed thinly with the crackle and roar from the burning interior. Molten lead dripped down from high upon the roofs in hot fiery gobs, as rafters and eaves blazed and burned. Waves of heat engulfed us and horses neighed with fear, their big eyes staring whitely. A presence hung in the air, foul and awesome and men were cowed to immobility and to silence.

The spell was broken by a harsh command. Horses' hooves again clattered on the cobblestones of the streets of Elgin as the marauders rode off. White faces peered at us from dark corners but there was no one to threaten our departure. We forded the River Lossie at Palmerscross and rode down the track towards Pluscarden, the hill-men padding tirelessly behind. A quick order sent a dozen bowmen ahead with a horse carrying the resin and as we rode up the valley the familiar flaming arches soared again, this time towards the high windows of the Abbey. Behind us, Elgin's agony glowed orange-red in the pale light of morning.

The hot excitement of the fight and of the flames was now over and the chilling damp of a fine drizzle of rain met us as we rode higher into the hills. Slung across a horse's back, I was desperately cold and uncomfortable. I had been imprisoned in the net for six hours. "Let me ride like a man, you swine," I shouted through my chattering jaws. "I can hardly escape from this rabble."

"Like a man?" roared the Wolf. "You young whelp of Bur's litter, you call yourself a man. When we get to Lochindorb I'll decide what to do wi yi. Meantime pray to God and be grateful you're not stuck through like a suckling pig."

The sun was past its zenith when we left the forests and the cold, white haar had vanished like steam from a pot. Up over the high moors we rode, past black tarns and peat bog, with the forest sliding from the valleys like smoke, and so to the bleak, bare shores of Lochindorb. I was stiff with cold. My feet felt lifeless and my fingers were numb. I was hefted on to the floorboards of a barge, amongst the hooves of the horses, then lifted bodily through the Watergate and to the dungeon.

Five

I must have lain on the stone floor of that pit for hours as life crept slowly back into me. The place was at least dry and warm. I was still trussed up in the net and it took me some time to pick the knots on the draw rope and free myself. I crept cautiously around in the blackness of my cell. I reckoned the place was near twelve feet square with no roof I could reach. There was a hole a span wide in the very middle of the stone floor and by the way the flags sloped towards the centre I guessed that this was the wash hole and the piss hole combined. I thought I could hear water lapping somewhere below me and gradually the faint glim of day came to me from the loch beneath.

"Why did you play the soldier? Two of you we had to kill but they are the only ones I trust. We came to burn not to slaughter." It was the second day of my imprisonment. I had been hefted out of the dungeon and now stood in a small panelled room in front of the Wolf. He was seated in a dark oak chair. It's strange the things one remembers. I remember the chair; it had lion feed and an embossed crown at the back above his head. The man in the chair was formidable. He was dressed in robes the colour of Spanish wine. His head was large. A mane of raven hair hung down to his neck, and his beard rested on his chest. But his eyes were what struck me and the slight droop of his left shoulder. In a flash I was back in the moonlight at the Lang Steps, my bowstring at my cheek and my arrow sighted towards the pale blur that was the face of a man on a black horse. I remembered how, with murder in my heart, I had only winged him. And then I saw the small round head of Chucker Bews rolling down towards the shingle.

"Does your left shoulder still pain you, Earl Buchan?"

The room became deadly silent.

"What is your name?"

"My name is Philip Hogeston and I am Laird of Plewlands. I last saw you at the Lang Steps."

"By Christ" said the Wolf, "The young whelp that winged me."

"A pity," I replied, my voice flat with rage, "that I failed to kill you."

There was a pause. Then his voice came slow and menacing.

"Well, well, this makes the situation much more interesting. Hogeston, is it? Right you hog. Jailer, cool this young hog's temper in the water pit."

The water pit was a disused well. The diameter of the shaft was some six feet and it was so fashioned that the water of the loch rose up the inside of the well shaft to a varying distance. Because it was the middle of summer the water reached the upper part of my thighs but in winter I had no doubt it would reach to a man's neck. The walls of the pit were slimy and, from the flagstones, which lined the bottom, to the top which was covered over like the dungeon, they rose thirteen feet. All this I learned in the hours I spent in that hellish place. Can you imagine what it is like to stand in icy water for six or ten hours at a time? The water came from near the cold bottom of the loch, which, just beyond the island, was twenty-five feet deep. At first I tried to keep the warmth in my legs by splashing about. This made me cold all over and wet, but at least it exercised me and prevented my feet becoming useless. I had no idea how long I was to be kept in that dungeon, but I knew after the first few hours that if I remained there much longer I would chill to death. If I took the weight off my feet, which I could do by sitting on the floor, the water lapped my neck. If I tried to float, I banged my head against the wall. I was, of course, in total darkness. By the distance I had fallen I reckoned there was some ten feet of well above me. I tried to climb the walls but there was no grip. The slimy covering made it impossible even to squeeze my fingers into crevices. A thin layer of sand covered the flags. This I scooped up and started to rub off the slime from part of the wall but I found to my despair that the cracks between the stones were too small.

After a long time, chilling to the bone, I had an idea. I am six feet tall and, with my arms extended, there was a full eight feet between my palms and the soles of my feet. By pressing my feet against one side of the wall and my hands against the other, surely I could spread eagle my way upwards. But first I had to get to work on the slime. It took me a long time to clear a swathe for both my hands and my feet. And then I discovered that by pressing against the walls in the upright position I could work my way up in a more comfortable fashion. After many attempts and many falls I felt my head bump against the lid of the well. Another six inches higher and I could, with a huge effort, just manage to balance the lid, which was heavy, on the top of my head and lift it sufficiently to see out. I heaved with my head and neck, but the effort was too much for my arms and, with a splash, I landed back in the water pit. Looking up, I could see a clear rim of light on one side of the lid. I gave myself some minutes to recover, half expecting that a guard would appear and find what I had done. Next time I reached the top I managed to nod the lid to the side, found my hands gripping the rim and, with a heave, I was on the flagged floor of a small courtyard under one of the corner towers of the Castle. I replaced the lid and dashed for the inner door.

I had no plan. I had not thought what I would do if I ever got free from that awful prison. My movements became the actions of a caged animal, and as ferocious. After that grim experience my one aim now was blind revenge. Face to face the Wolf had shrunk to human size. It was true that he had an enormous head and a thick body but his height was less than mine and he was more than twice my age.

Covered in slime from the water pit I slunk through the corridors and stairs of the Castle, like a water kelpie. It was strangely easy. I was the hunter, downwind from my quarry. No one in the Castle expected an intruder. No one was on guard. Outside, the long summer twilight gleamed in the North-west but inside, the Castle was in half gloom and the lanterns were unlit. From a distance came the sound of laughter and the soft twanging of a harp, a door opened and the sounds swelled down the corridor. I slid out of sight into a room. Someone came towards me along the passage, the door flew open and the Wolf stepped inside. I had my hands on his neck a split second before he recognised me but not before he shouted "Hawk." My onslaught took him to the floor and his hands were on my face and in my hair. Pain exploded in my gut and I felt the breath going out of me. I gasped for air and my lungs deflated in a long sobbing cry. I sensed rather than saw the foot lifting again to kick my face but the shattering blow never came.

"Back Hawk," the Wolf ordered and I was hefted like a sack of malt from the floor, thrown against a wall and held there by pressure on my throat.

"So monk, you thought to have another go at me, and failed again." His voice was soft and threatening.

"My God you'll pay for this. Hawk, take this hog, this young boar to the peat bog. I will dispose of you as I dispose of unwanted rubbish."

The Hawk took charge of me. He was a gnome-like creature with a face which lacked a nose and ears. He had dreamy eyes and slack lips. The Wolf sat back on a bed and studied me. His face in the glow of sunset looked older than I expected and pendulous ear-lobes hung down almost to the angles of his jaw.

"On second thoughts, my murderous monk I can use you, I think."

My breath was coming back and my groaning had ceased. A terrible pain gripped my belly and I vomited without warning straight into the Hawk's ugly face.

"Yes, you confused bastard of a warrior monk, I can use you. I appoint you priest to the Wolf of Badenoch." He gave a roar of laughter. "By God I've got you, you vindictive viper. Chaplain to the Wolf of Badenoch," and another gust of laughter shook his big frame. "Chaplain to the Devil your Bishop will say!"

I was frog-marched by the Hawk to another part of the Castle and pushed into a room which was very different from the dungeons which had been my lot in the past few days. This was a circular room and I knew that it must be at the top of one of the corner towers of the Castle. The Hawk threw me forward on to a paved floor and for good measure booted me between the legs. The pain was so searing that I must have lain in a heap on the floor for long enough. It was dark when I opened my eyes and crawled on to a low bed, slime, damp, blood and all.

Six

I was imprisoned in that room for two days and nights, never seeing nor hearing a soul but the curlews quavering and the tiny songs of the larks. In those lonely hours, as the sun moved high overhead and night snatched but three hours to itself, a battle raged inside my head. It horrifies me still to recall the mad fury that overwhelmed me. Locked like a wild beast in this small cage I beat the door till my knuckles bled. I rattled on the window bars until my palms blistered, and I shouted curses till my voice broke and my breath came in huge sobs. Self pity it was and black hate of the Wolf of Badenoch. And so I lay the second night quivering and babbling like a madman on that straw bed. I excuse myself now by wishing up some simple explanation for those days of desperation. I had a fever after my hours in the water pit. Thirst had made me mad – perhaps, or perhaps not.

I awoke the second morning, my head cool and my thoughts rational. I rose and looked through the grilled windows of my cell. To the North stretched the forest of Darnaway. East, through a gap in the hills, was the valley of the Spey. To the South-west I could look towards the Grampian Mountains and the endless moors that reached the Monadhliaths. I lay on my bed, and, for the first time, I saw the figure. I was astonished I had not noticed it before. Perhaps my hate blinded me to anything of such beauty. It hung on the wall near a lamp and when the sun rose from the hills above the Spey I knew that this was the North wall. Like the others it was curved and the early morning sun bathed the carving with pure cold light. At noon the mid-day rays, clear and all pervading, exposed every detail, and in the long evening it was caressed by the soft magnolia light of dusk, which made it so unbearably alive as to bring starts of tears to my eyes. When I saw it first my heart leapt and I gazed in astonishment at this strange and lovely carving. The man who hung from the cross wore no halo or crown of thorns. The nails that pierced his hands were real nails and he was totally naked. He was young with tight curly hair and he held his head up strongly in a position of keen awareness.[4] During that day I examined the carving minutely. It was made of painted wood. The colours were delicate enough but it owed its beauty and arresting power to the curve of the naked body, to the challenge in the set of the head, and especially, to the strong masculinity of the man. His eyes were not the sad blank eyes of the usual Christ on the Cross. They looked straight into my face and their message was like a shout: "I have survived even this."

It was evening when I heard the door closing gently. I turned swiftly. A bundle lay on the floor. The door opened easily but there was no sight or sound of any living person. I stood with my back against it and shook like a branch of acacia. I was deadly tired, sick, cold and still damp from the water pit. I stripped off my filthy clothes, pulled on the long grey shirt that now lay by the door, and tumbled into sleep. When I awoke on the third morning a pitcher of water sat in a large tub and towelling hung on a chair. Clean clothes and the cowelled robe of a white monk had been mysteriously provided. My sword, belt, helm, dagger and targe were stacked neatly under the sculpture, cleaned and business-like. When I saw them I cried out in joy. Someone in this grim prison was on my side and escape was possible. I picked up my dagger. The feel of it gave me hope and its sharp double edge and needle point renewed the killing-flush. That dagger was my reward for challenging and slaying the enemy of a young French nobleman who was afraid to risk his own perfumed skin. The blade was as wicked a piece of steel as you could hope to possess. But the real attraction was in the hilt. As I held it, my fingers grasped and caressed the smooth ivory figure of a naked girl. For this dagger I had killed a stranger.

I was standing thus before the carved Christ. I looked up. My eyes locked with those of the young man on the Cross and the heat of hate became a flush of embarrassment. There rushed to my ears the angry scornful words flung at me by the Wolf.

"What are you? Monk or murderer?"

"Escape, escape" sang my heart's blood. I grasped the dagger tightly and descended the turret stair. Early morning light bathed the small courtyard. The portcullis was up and there was no sight or sound of the guard. I ran towards the gate. A pair of oyster catchers "peep-peeped" and over the water, a quarter of a mile away in the woods, I saw a horse, saddled and bridled. A small boat fretted on its painter and gently nudged the open watergate. I waited, listening. Were there men above me with spears poised? Would an arrow flight its deadly way to my breast as I rowed out into the loch? But all I heard was the lapping of small waves on the castle wall. There was no one to stop me, no one but myself and at that moment I knew I was trapped in this Castle of Lochindorb as surely as if the portcullis had crashed down in from of me. Trapped by my own pride, my curiosity? Perhaps. I had never run away and there was more, much more, to learn of this Devil man who had shouted at me three nights ago, "What are you? Monk or murderer?" Was I trapped by my jailer? Maybe. But the decision was my own. If I made the easy choice – the boat, the horse and freedom – I would never know if I was a man of valour or a man of straw; a prudent man or a coward.

"I give you the opportunity," my jailer was saying. "The opportunity to know yourself." Or was it the naked man nailed to the wooden cross who had spoken to me? My mind was made up. I flung the ivory handled woman-knife high over the quicksilver loch. It vanished, and my heart sang its relief. Far from being a captive in this island fortress I felt free like a lark in the blue sky.

During that whole day only the Hawk visited me, his face inscrutable; and with him, food, a good helping of venison pie and a mug of cool ale. The following day I was summoned to meet the Wolf.

I had been expecting this confrontation and had in my mind a bold, concise speech which would clearly explain why I had chosen to stay. But when I arrived I found myself at a family supper party. All five sons were there with their mother and father, as well as others of the family and a group of friends. The face I knew best was that of old MacShimie who had ridden the long miles from Beaufort Castle beyond Inverness. A splendid cloak of russet cloth gave bulk to his small frame as he hoped it would, but the bald head bobbing on top spoiled the effect and made him look like a shuttle-cock. I recognised the Duke of Atholl and his lady, and Sir Hugh Menzies of Comrie Castle with his two daughters. It was a glittering array and I was grudgingly compelled to admit it. Set in a Wolf's lair it was worthy of a King's son. To entertain us were three harpists, two minstrels and a jester. Only he took any notice of my entrance and capered up to me as I walked towards the table. No one showed the least surprise when I entered or, in fact, any interest whatsoever, but a voice commanded, "The grace, Chaplain, give the grace." In Latin I prayed that the Grace of Christ would settle upon all, even those who could expect nothing of God's forgiving mercy. There was a low chuckle from the Wolf and then a solemn "Amen." "This is the villainous priest," he said loudly to his guests, "who has twice tried to murder me. We shall see soon who is the stronger, the hog or the Wolf!"

The jester appeared at my elbow, his flattened face in comic contrast to the yellow-fanged wolf-mask nodding on his left shoulder. "Drink to that, drink to that, priest" he said. He raised a goblet, chanted a parody of the sacrament and emptied the wine into the gaping jaws of the wolf's head lolling on his shoulder. There was a roar of laughter and then another as the implication of the mime was understood. He was gone in a trice, leaping and capering down the hall to shouts of encouragement, his fox tails and leather jesses flicking in all directions, his bells jangling like a miniature cathedral. His face was covered in a white paste, but I recognised the Hawk. My opinion of the vacant moron who had torn me from his master's throat four nights ago suffered a swift revision. Here were talent, brain and cunning. Then, I would have found it impossible to believe I could have shared even a gesture of human sympathy with that deformed creature, yet in the weeks that followed he was my only visitor. He made a habit of arriving suddenly and silently just after dawn and he would squat for some minutes inside the room. His pale lustreless eyes would take in the surroundings, myself, and finally the figure on the Cross. He would gaze steadily at the smitten man, his brute mouth slack. I was soon convinced that this regular appearance at dawn had begun long before my occupation of that little room and that far from resenting my presence there, he was, in his silent way, pleased to be sharing him with me. No word was exchanged between us but I soon lost the feeling of annoyance his appearance caused at first, and it came to me that by sharing these moments I was gaining a friend in this friendless place. No one else came near me. The servants quickened their steps and disappeared at my approach. Men in Roman-style woollen kilts and leather brogues, short hacking swords at their sides, shied away from me as if fearful of their master's anger.

It was a month before I was ordered to appear again before the family. On this occasion I was led to a room quite different from the others I had seen. It was high in the central tower and the windows, although small, were not the narrow embrasures of a fortress. The walls were painted in whitewash, the slate floor polished jet-black with soot, the furniture rich and tapestried. The Wolf stood at the farthest window and gazed out over the Loch. Beside him sat his eldest son Alexander, a tall red-headed man barely my own age. From my left a hard young voice spoke, "Priest, where are your manners?" I looked towards the speaker and hostility slashed at me across the room. James Stewart, third son of the Wolf of Badenoch, spat the words.

"Ignore my mother at your peril."

I wrenched my eyes from his. Behind him on a low chair sat a woman. All the tales I had heard of this Jezebel, this painted whore, this kept woman of the Earl of Buchan, danced through my head and the flush on my neck swooped high to my face. She was strikingly handsome. Her face was perfectly oval, her brow high, her cheekbones moulded by Viking ancestry. I had read in poems of the swan-like neck and the description fitted, her slender neck expanding into soft round shoulders. She sat quite motionless on the couch and hair of palest wheat cascaded the whole length of her back. Commanded by more than young James's bold voice I strode towards her, lifted her long slim fingers to my lips. The words were out before reason could stop them.

"Princess Mariota," I said, "I am honoured to meet you."

"Spoken more like a gentleman than a monk," said the Wolf. Then from James, "Where did you get your prissy manners? Do they teach you etiquette and deportment at the Sang School?" He strode across the room to stand three feet from me, glaring straight into my eyes. In one swift movement his mother was between us. "Don't let there be any bickering," she said. "We have brought you here priest, for a special purpose. Our son Andrew is ill and we need your prayers." She turned to her oldest son. "Come with me Sandy and we'll take our chaplain to Andrew's bedroom."

Andrew's room was some distance away. It was small and full of the trinkets and treasures of the young teenager. A bear-skin rug covered the floor, but the bear's head had been thrust out of sight under a chair. When we were all inside we could hardly turn. Andrew lay under sheep skins on a cot. His face was the colour of wood-ash and glistened with sweat. His lips were pale lilac. His breath rasped in his throat and tainted the stuffy room with a musty fetor. It was a smell that brought back memories. I remembered my mother kneeling beside a sick child. She had been younger than Andrew, but her illness had stamped on her face the same frightened, anxious look that Andrew now had, and the smell was the same. Four days later a sad little procession had moved from Plewlands to Ogistoun Kirk and my younger sister was buried. I remembered too how my mother had burned all her clothes and toys, even her plates, and how every day for at least a fortnight she had shooed the rest of us out of the house and ordered us to play as long as light remained in the sky. The harsh gasping sound in Andrew's throat filled the small room. Lady Mariota knelt before him, just like my mother so many years ago. I looked at his brother Alexander. The hard manly look had gone and his face was soft. His mother rose and faced me.

"Well?" she asked.

"Lady Mariota," I said, "I have seen this before. It is the croup." I dug in my memory for some words of advice. "Andrew must be nursed in a larger room, a room with a fire so that the air is kept pure. A bucket of water should be steaming at his bedside. My sister had this illness many years ago, and I remember she breathed easier in the steam of her bathtub."[5]

"And your prayers, priest?"

"Yes, I will pray for him, but do as I suggest."

All that my mother had done for my sister had failed to save her. I asked for the same to be done for this boy Andrew, and, by some miracle, he lived.

When Andrew was on his feet for the first time, weak and giddy, but happy, I found my position in the Castle of Lochindorb changed for the better. To say I had become part of the family would be an exaggeration. They were close, and guarded their privileges tightly. Yet I was not now looked upon as some peculiar piece of machinery to be wound up at their pleasure. The contagion did not spread, not even to the baby. The Wolf and Mariota had six children. Margaret, the youngest, during Andrew's illness, was nursed in the Croft of Auchtertipper by Hilda McDonnell, Mariota's maid. Alexander was the oldest and held himself aloof from his brothers, Walter, James and Duncan. I saw less of Duncan than the rest. He was as tough and as predatory as his father. At that time he was fifteen, and for a year he had led a wild band of robbers in Glenshee.

Walter and James were only too glad to be ordered off to net the salmon. It had been a wet August and the rivers were high. Fish had steadily moved up the streams since February and the pools between Knockando and Grantown were filled with salmon. The boys loved it. They would set off at dusk with their ghillies, saddlebags packed with net and line, and I often went with them. We staked the net across the neck of a big pool, weighted it down and allowed it to belly out into the river beyond. Wooden floats, tied on to the upper rope of the net, showed us how it lay and when well placed it allowed no salmon to move from the pool into the rapids above. We would settle down for the night somewhere, light a fire and sleep under the stars. When dawn came four hours later and the night mists over the river started to melt away, we stood at the tail of the pool, shouted and yelled, and threw boulders into the river. One end of the net was released and pulled towards the opposite shore hard and fast so as to turn it inside out and drag the struggling fish towards the bank. We seldom left the river at breakfast time without at least five good salmon strung across our ponies' backs. There was one memorable night when we landed twenty. We picked ten, the medium size are always the best eating, and left the rest for the otters.

When I went on these trips with Walter and James, I discarded my monk's cloak and donned the leather jerkin and woollen trews that the boys wore. Our two ghillies were friendly lads, slightly younger than myself, whose characters expanded once they were free from the eyes and ears of the Wolf. Peter Grant, in particular, one of the Castle butchers, enjoyed these all-night expeditions with the young Stewarts. He was, and still is, a powerful man with the strong arms of his trade, and wrestler's shoulders. I was a useful wrestler myself and Grant and I would set about each other in mock earnest in the heather. The boys took sides and the hills around echoed their yells of encouragement and scorn. I was quicker on my feet and perhaps slightly sharper in my reactions, but Peter was so powerful that once he had me in his grip I was in trouble. Although my ability to feint could catch him out, neither of us had much of an edge on the other. Big Walt the slaughterman came with us often, a handsome giant, well over six feet tall, broad chested and with a big head set like a rock on his shoulders. He was a gentle fellow, slaughterers and hangmen often are, with striking features that should have made him a stallion among the women. His heavy moustaches drooped beyond the corners of his mouth, his whiskers arched forward to his cheekbones and his brown, thick hair was trimmed to the neck of his jerkin. He had soft solemn eyes and, in these days, he seldom laughed.

They were fun, those nights in the forests or high among the hills. Both Walt and Peter were born story-tellers. Walt's tales were all of disaster and misfortune. Peter's were breezy and lighthearted. Wrapped in our plaids by a glowing campfire, the dying light mourned by the curlews and the belling of stags, they would recount their tales of witches and warlocks, and of the ancient hunters. As darkness welled into the sky, the stars appeared. On moonless nights, so bright they wheeled, so sharp they shone, the boys would stretch their arms to touch them. Then in their Highland tongues, the ghillies would tell the tale of the giant in the Southern sky with his faithful hound at heel; stories of the Great Bear in the North, of the Seven Sisters and of the Merry Dancers.

I was twenty-one years old and when I think on it the boys were not much younger. Alexander was a year or two my junior although he would not have admitted it. I liked "Sandy". He had all the arrogance of the Royal Blood but with it, the common touch so many true aristocrats can simulate. Like all the Wolf's sons he was suspicious of my presence, but as the story of the defence of the Cathedral leaked out from the sculleries of the castle he became as friendly as his wary nature would allow. He spent most of the year at the court of his uncle King Robert III, known in the family as "hirplin' Johnny", because he was christened John and was an ineffectual, gentle cripple though King of Scotland and grandson of The Bruce. Sandy had travelled widely, not only to London, but to France in the company of Sir Robert Grant, his neighbour, ambassador to the French court. Sandy was a born soldier. He told me an army would fight as its soldiers were accustomed to fighting and not necessarily as their captains expected them to. When he boasted that one day he intended to lead Scotland's Army he no more than told the truth. He was ambitious and supported his father's quarrel with Bishop Bur simply for what his father could get. Any retrenchment of the Wolf's authority was like a goad in Sandy's side and in this, he resembled his brother Duncan who took such matters to a more literal conclusion.

Walter, a year younger than Sandy, was a practical fellow. If one compared Walter's room with Sandy's it was like comparing a stable to a byre. Sandy's was littered with knives, half-cleaned stag horns, boar's teeth and birds' eggs, while Walter's was a model of good order. Unlike Sandy's his collection of eggs was properly arranged and labelled. He was writing a natural history of the birds and beasts of Badenoch, an interest which suited him for the office of steward his father had given him. To those inferiors whom he trusted he was civil and generous, but woe betide the thief. Some beasts went missing from a small herd at Dulsie on the river Findhorn. Walter was determined to find them and came upon the stolen cattle at the croft of Coig-na-fearn in the Monadhliath mountains near the source of the river. Only two were Lochindorb cattle but because they were stolen Walter strung up the thief by the neck to his own lintel. He turned to the screaming wife, babe on her back and, speaking to his men, said, "Wench and brat are tarred wi' the same brush. Now they can thieve for themselves, but not from me."

James, the youngest of the three, was quite different from his brothers. He was a surly-faced lad with a dour nature. At sixteen he was taller than either Sandy or Walter but lean and spindly. When I was alone with him he ignored me completely. Only when we were in the company of Peter Grant or Big Walt was I tolerated or was my presence acknowledged. And then, he made it perfectly clear that in his estimation I was inferior to the slaughter-men. Monks were beyond his contempt, an attitude he had taken from his father who missed no opportunity to miscry the church. James's superior indifference to me was irritating to say the least. Once, angered more than usual, I called him a conceited pup and had my face spat upon. Peter Grant, with a twinkle in his eye, described the incident as "a whit embarrassing but you asked for it! James is like the loch he lives on, cold and deep and dangerous."

Peter Grant had two stories the lads liked him to tell. He never retold a story in exactly the same way. There was always some subtle difference, something missed out. This would be done quite deliberately and the younger boys, were quick to correct him. We lay once in a cave above Tulchan. It was high up on the side of a hill and looked directly to the North and West. On that clear night you could see the mountains beyond the Moray Firth, Ben Wyvis, and the sharp peaks beyond the Great Glen. Mile upon mile of undulating moorland glowed in the evening light. The heather was in bloom and the whole of Scotland seemed cloaked in purple.

"Have you ever been South of the Grampian?" Peter began and continued, "I have once, away down by the Garry and the Tilt and the Tummel and the Tay, and do you know that the trees there are one hundred feet high and the forests are dark as night." He pointed towards the sunset.

"Have you ever thought why it is we have no forests North of Badenoch? Well, I will tell ye. It was all the fault of the King of Norroway, ten Kings before Haakon, whom my great-grandfather fought at the Battle of Largs." According to Peter all his people had been chiefs of the clan and all were fighters.

"And when this Haakon sailed his ships from the islands in the North he grew very envious of the fine forests and the straths that we have in Scotland. He was displeased that he and his wild men were never welcome there, so he sent his old nurse all the way from Norroway to Cape Wrath. She was a witch and could make herself invisible and she hid in the clouds and rained down spears of fire on the forests beneath her. In the month of August they were like dried tinder, and they burned and burned and it was not long before all the woods, all the timber, was in flames and nothing but charred trunks stood between Cape Wrath and the Findhorn. It was very serious. Indeed it was. Well, the wise men of Badenoch, and there were many wise men in Badenoch, gathered at the standing stones of Kingussie and worked at a plan how they could defeat the witch. And this is what they did. They herded all the sheep and all the cattle and all the pigs from Dallas in the North to Insch in the South. And when they had gathered them together they separated off the lambs from the ewes, the calves from the cows, the young hogs from the sows, and the foals from the mares. The noise that the young animals made and the noise that their mothers made when they found themselves separated from their young was something fearful and the old witch up in the huge smoke-cloud, wondering what could be the matter, stuck her head out of the cloud, och, just for a few moments, to see. And when she did, the men of Badenoch shot her full of arrows. And so the forests of Ballochbuie, the forest of Marr and the forest of Rothiemurchus and the forest of Glenmore were all saved."

Another witch story was about the famous hunter, Weelam. "Weelam was netting salmon at the Pot of Sourden, the deep swirling pool on the River Spey below Rothes and this witch was gathering toadstools and frogs on the far side. It was growing dark when she slipped and fell straight into the Sourden Pot, where she would have drowned, of course, because witches can not live in water, had she not stuck in Weelam's net. He pulled her to the far shore where she lay gasping on the sands. Weelam, seeing that she was a witch, said 'I will throw you right back into the Sourden pot if you do not grant me one wish.' The witch, still wrapped in his net, was terrified and said she would grant him anything he wanted. Now Weelam was not only a fisherman but a skilled hunter, and so he asked the witch for the one thing which the hunter could best be without. He told her to take his scent from him. This made him the most successful hunter that ever was, because the stags could not smell him and he could creep closer to them than any man."

The boys laughed at the funny parts of these tales, or looked solemn and wise but Big Walt never smiled. I knew, of course, that he had a problem, and waited for him to bring it into the open. When at last he did, we were at Ruthven Castle whence the family had moved in the late summer to hunt stag. One morning early, Peter Grant, Big Walt and I climbed to the slopes of Sgoran Dubh. The night mist poured up the hillsides and vanished when the sun touched it. We sat in the heather and chewed cold pig's trotters. Suddenly Walt spoke. "Pheelip," he said, "Have you ever had a woman?" He sat, hunched, on a round rock, staring gloomily down at Loch Einich, as it unveiled, two thousand feet below.

"Why do you ask?" I parried. "Should I not? I may be of the Church, but I am a man first."

"Aye, and that's why I asked you. Did you – was she pleased – with what you did to her?"

"Why, yes. I was pretty pleased myself."

"How do you know she was pleased?"

"Well, for one thing she told me so. And for another, she wasn't slow to want it again. Has no girl ever shown her pleasure to you Walt?" I asked gently.

"Och, aye," he replied, but without conviction. I waited. "Pheelip," he said, "I canna tell you a lee. I just dinna ken. I used to think I was a rare bull wi' the women. But now – I'm nae so sure."

"Why, Walt?" Peter broke in, "Are you not big enough?"

"I don't know," replied Walt, his big spaniel eyes and long handsome face a picture of dejection. Wisps of wind rose from the Loch. An eagle soared out a hundred feet below, wings stiff, primaries feeling the air like gentle fingers on a lute.

"He's taken to eating bullock's baas," said Peter dolefully. "That's hoo bad he is."

"Is that true Walt?"

"Of course it's true," growled Peter. "The feel cratur'll mak hissel ill." Across the moorland a golden plover called to his love. The sun was warm on our backs, and soft airs fanned the hot smell of granite.

"Och. Stop worrying Walt. It'll not help. What you need is a douce wee wifie to love you and nae mair o' thon shallow enthusiastic birds you've been messing wi' from Elgin." Peter Grant has said it better than I could. A load had lifted from Walt and his eyes brightened. We had a stiff walk ahead. The stags were in a corrie above us and we had to move them gently down to the waiting huntsmen.

Sandy seldom came with us in these expeditions. I think that he felt he would lose his dignity. However, one September evening he announced suddenly that he was going fishing and he would take with him anyone who wanted to come. He well knew that we were going fishing that night, and this was just his way of asserting his authority. We all set out together in the pink light of the September sunset, climbed the hill to the West of Chorrach, rode across the watershed of the Upper Dorbach, gave Castle Grant a wide berth, and reached the fine pool in the River Spey below Cromdale. That was one of the few nights in which we caught nothing. Our dawn haul netted a surprised and snapping otter, but no fish. This so infuriated Sandy that he leapt into the shallows and clubbed the otter viciously.

"For why did your do that, Lord Sandy?" asked Peter simply. "There's plenty more salmon in the Spey and plenty more nights."

In a towering rage Sandy led us back towards Lochindorb. It was scarcely light and cloud hung closely to the surface of the river. The bracken was wet with dew and our horses' tracks showed up as dark paths through the misted green. We had no difficulty in picking up the tracks of a fairly large herd of cattle being driven down the valley towards the Spey at Grantown. If Sandy hadn't been so put out by our luckless night he would have thought nothing of it, but he took it into his head that these were stolen cattle belonging to his father and were being driven down to Castle Grant. And for all we knew he might have been right. We came upon them near Delliefure. There were some forty head of cattle with ten or fifteen calves, and eleven mounted herdsmen, all armed. Thinking it was a fool's ploy Walter and James and I held back, and Sandy and the two ghillies were in the midst of the robbers before they knew what was happening. Sandy's bold charge scattered them but they were on him immediately and, to our dismay, we saw him dragged to the ground under a mob of struggling men. The two ghillies leapt to his aid but were quickly overwhelmed. To join the fight would have been madness so we turned our horses and rode pell-mell back to Lochindorb for help.

When we told the Wolf what had happened he was furious and within minutes a war party was being rowed across to the mainland. He refused to let James and Walter go with him, but I had been in charge and, therefore, I would ride with him "and be bartered for the missing men".

By the time the sun was properly up we were past Craigliath and thundering on towards Castle Grant. It was there we met Sandy, galloping towards us, black rage in every feature, his right arm hanging at his side and his shoulder clotted with blood. He reined in his horse and spoke to his father. "The ghillies are in the dungeon," he said, "and the cattle are all penned below the Castle."

"Are you certain they are ours?" asked his father.

"As sure as I can be," said Sandy. "But Robert Grant says they are his."

Sir Robert Grant was the Wolf's nearest neighbour and until then they had been friends. He was the King's Ambassador to the Court in France and he and his wife Matilda had supped at Lochindorb only a month previously. The arrival of the Wolf at Castle Grant so soon on the heels of Sandy's departure took him completely by surprise. The guards at the keep were overpowered and the Wolf burst straight into the courtyard.

"Sir Robert," he cried, "Come down and talk or I'll burn you out of your pigeon holes as I have burned the Bishop of Moray." Down came Sir Robert, himself in a towering rage, and the two men stood and glared at each other while the matter of the stolen cattle was debated by their stewards.

"Stolen be damned," said Sir Robert, "They're my own beasts."

The two men stamped out of the Castle and down to the folds. Sure enough there wasn't a single beast of Lochindorb's in the herd. What could the Wolf say?

"Free my ghillies and I'll forget the matter."

"You can have your ghillies but I'm damned if I'll forget the matter," shouted Sir Robert, and the two men parted in a blaze of fury.

I can tell you the ghillies were very glad to see us again. They had been thrown into Castle Grant's notorious dungeon where, had we not arrived so early, they would have been hung up with hooks through their ankles like meat carcasses to rot for ever as cattle thieves.

Seven

Although a big change had taken place in my status in the Lochindorb household, I had not forgotten the horrors of the Seventeenth of June and the wild battle in the early morning mists of St. Botolph's Day. I was anxious to know the fate of my companions, and what had happened to the Cathedral, if it still stood or if it had been burnt to the ground. In the early days of my captivity I demanded an answer to these questions.

"But for your vain piece of swordsmanship there would have been no casualties and nothing left of the Cathedral," was the Wolf's retort. Later he had called me to his room.

"You were asking about your friends, priest. Two of them are dead but the other one, the one who was with you at the gate, is still alive. Bishop Bur has sent such a list of damage to the Pope and to the King that it will cost as much to repair as it cost to build the place. We struck your bloated priests a fine body blow, and now that they have been driven out of their snug burrows, perhaps, although it is too much to expect, perhaps they will start looking after their people."

During Andrew's illness I overheard other things that made me wonder. The boy was much improved. Steaming water softened by herbs sat close to the bedside at all times. I recognised the bowl as the Bishop's chalice for which Chucker Bews had died that autumn night at the Bay of the Primroses. Of the rest of the stolen treasure I saw no sign although I had little doubt that most, if not all of it, had been melted to make ornaments, plates and goblets.

Lady Mariota taunted me openly once in front of her husband.

"Do you ever repent your folly Philip Hogeston?" she asked. "Do you still think the rich baubles of your church worthy of the death of a friend?" The Wolf's shoulder which I had pierced with my arrow five years before caused him frequent pain and I guessed that the latter was the cause of Lady Mariota's exasperation. Her blue eyes were fixed on mine. Scorn was in her voice and in the turn of her mouth.

"Do you know what has become of the candlesticks blessed by your Pope's avaricious fingers?"

"Yes," I replied. "They are debased to ornaments and table-ware for the use of the ungodly." Out of the corner of my eye I saw the Wolf take a swift step in my direction, then a glance from Mariota stopped him. Slowly, watching me with a cat-smile on her lips, she moved her hands over her breasts and turned as in a dance, hips and thighs undulating like the vibrant notes of a harp. Circling her waist was a golden belt, its bands plaited in the sensuous intricacy of the love-knot. She faced me again. Where her thighs met her stomach the glittering jewel ended in a pair of wild-cat, tails entwined.

"Beauty is akin to godliness. Do you not agree, Hog?" said the Wolf.

I looked at him. He stood in his arrogant way, big head tilted slightly, a mocking smile in his eyes.

"Can you suggest a better use for your ornaments priest?"

On another occasion I was sitting with Andrew while he played with soldiers his brother James had fashioned from clay. James had a macabre imagination and his tableaux of painted warriors included limbless and headless corpses in abundance. The Earl and his lady came in to the room talking.

"If the King insists that you receive the lady Euphemia you will have to do so."

"Have to?" exclaimed the Wolf. "We parted company eight years ago. You are my wife Mariota, since before Sandy was born and will be, God willing, until I die." Suddenly he saw me.

"Hog, how's your invalid? Christ help you if he dies!" Not waiting for an answer, he talked quietly to Andrew. Between his bouts of ill-humour he could be kind, and to this sick child, as to all his sons, he was indeed a prince.

Since I was taken to Lochindorb he had engaged in few forays but his second son, Duncan, was less restrained. His father's successful assaults on the town of Forres and Elgin had inspired him to attempt similar raids South and West of the Grampian Mountains. By this time, the Wolf's lawless acts had forfeited him his title of "Justiciar North of the Forth" and justified though it was, this angered him and enraged Duncan. The loss to his father of powerful legal rights did not deter that wild young man. He built a thieves' nest in the mountains above Brechin from where he descended by the valleys of the Isla, the South Esk, the North Esk, or the Dee, on the fat lands in the Mearns and on the trade routes South from Aberdeen. His robber band was at last caught and badly mauled by Sir Walter Ogilvie, Sheriff of Angus, Sir Patrick Gray and Sir David Lindsay of Glenesk, all past victims of Duncan's raids, who ambushed him at Gasklune. They paid dearly who tangled with the Highlanders. Sixty men they lost and their leader, Walter Ogilvie, but Duncan's force was so weakened that he rode West over the Grampians with those who survived and returned to Lochindorb to lick his wounds.

Not long afterwards a King's Herald arrived at the island Fortress. He was Robert Douglas, son of James, Lord Balvenie, and he brought to the Wolf a summons from the King to appear before him at his Court in Aberdeen on pain of death.

I was with the family when Robert Douglas arrived.

There was silence as the Wolf read the missive.

"By God, Robert," he exclaimed. "If you were not the son of my friend James Douglas I would have you thrown into the Water Pit. Do you know what this" –he waved the parchment with its heavy seal contemptuously above his head- "What this legal rubbish says?"

"Yes, Lord Buchan," he replied. "It pains me to convey it to you, and I am presuming on our friendship to save me from your anger. I have to impress on you, however, that the King will brook no denial."

"My brother John shows more spirit than I gave him credit for. So! I have to answer these charges, have I? Firstly – and I can see old sour-face Bur behind this – 'to crave forgiveness and promise substantial compensation for the burning of the Cathedral and Episcopal property at Elgin'. Forgiveness indeed! I'll see Bur to Hell first! Secondly, the old story, 'to return to thy lawful place as spouse to Euphemia Countess of Ross'. Can't my fool of a brother get it into his thick head that my marriage to that barren, scheming bitch is over for good! And thirdly – Ho, Ho, Master Duncan, here we have it, - 'to deliver my son Duncan Stewart to the provost and magistrates of the Town of Aberdeen, and to the deputy sheriff of Angus, for trial. The charges against him are: One, his wanton and unprovoked attacks upon the lands between Forfar and Aberdeen, and on persons therein. Two, the destruction of valuable property within the burgh of Aberdeen' – valuable property be damned, there's not a house or croft in that town worth a Scots merk. 'Three, the murder within the burgh lands of Thomas Webster and James Lorimer' – what the Devil, Duncan! What say you to this?"

Duncan, who had been lolling unconcerned by this catalogue of crime, sat up with a start.

"Killed in fair fight my Lord," he exclaimed. "Murdo McInnes and Peter Grant were challenged in an alehouse."

The Wolf glowered, then rose to his feet. "Brother John commands my appearance on pain of Death, does he! I'll teach him to meddle in my affairs. Send for McInnes."

The dark, burly, straggle-haired captain of the fortress appeared. He and I had no liking for each other.

"McInnes," roared the Wolf. "Mount one hundred horse. Send to Ruthven, Balvenie, Auchindoun, Strathbogie, Castle Grant and Rothes. Seek the company, on a visit to the King in Aberdeen, of Douglas, Gordon, Grant and Leslie. Send a rider to Irvine of Drum on the river Dee and ask if he will receive us in ten days from now."

While the King fidgeted and fretted in Aberdeen, awaiting, with his court, the arrival of his penitent brother, Alexander, Earl of Buchan, descended the valley of the river Dee with two hundred armed knights, warriors, sons and servants. I was included in the cavalcade. As the Wolf said, "It will surprise the Bishop of Moray, and any surprise, even you Hog, is worth a troop of mounted men." He slapped me on the shoulder with great good humour. He was at his best preparing for action. His designs were always on a broad canvas. He and he alone had to hold the centre of the scene and the character he played had to be larger than life. He had no time for the subtleties. His actions, sometimes devious, were always majestic. This adventure was heady wine to him for the prospect of confronting his brother the King and his old adversary Bishop Bur presented the sort of challenge he was born to accept. A trap it might be – he was under the shadow of excommunication and any man could be his executioner – but the Wolf had a nose for danger and double dealing. Sandy and Duncan came with us, of course, and Walter and James also. Andrew was too young and not sufficiently recovered from the croup to travel and stayed at Lochindorb with his little sister Margaret. For the two youngest boys it was all excitement and fun. They rode their ponies amongst the horsemen, skelped the rumps of the pack-horses laden with fresh salmon and new-killed venison, or sat proudly out in front. Our journey took two nights and two days. We rested and changed mounts at Castle Craig near Rhynie and arrived on the evening of the second day at Drum Castle on the River Dee. Five years before, Irvine of Drum and the Earl of Buchan and Badenoch had travelled together to treat with the Emir of Acre for the ransom of six Scottish knights. The two men were old friends and Irvine had arranged for our comfort.

On the tenth day after he had received the Royal Summons the Wolf of Badenoch arrived at the gates of Aberdeen, preceded by the King's Herald, at the head of two hundred and thirty armed horsemen. As we emerged from the leafy valley of the river Dee, banners flying, pennants fluttering and helmets glinting in the sunlight, we must have been a fearsome sight to the guards on the City wall. At our head rode the Wolf, his war-flag, the red lion rampant on azure and silver, streaming in the East wind. We entered by the Hardgate and were met there by the Provost and Magistrates. Our horses' hooves clattered on the cobblestones as we rode through the town to the Gallowgate and then by Spitalhill to the Chanonry where we were to be lodged. We heard the cry "The Wolf! The Wolf of Badenoch!" shouted up the closes and the narrow wynds and folk tumbled out to glower and to gape, for the spectacle of the Earl of Buchan and Lord of Badenoch trooping his banners through the streets of Aberdeen was not to be missed.

The King had hastily arranged quarters out of the town for our unexpectedly large party, and, to take the heat out of the situation, he commanded us to join him at High mass that afternoon in the Machiar Kirk. I found myself at the altar attending on the Bishop of Glasgow and St Andrews, while my old master, Bishop Bur glared at me across the aisle. I doubt if the Church of St. Machiar has ever seen such a gathering. The Stewart stood aside to allow the King and his knights to enter, less, I thought from politeness, than to enable him to leave first and to arm up ahead of his adversaries.

The confrontation occurred the following day. We marched from the Chanonry to the Castle, and the folk of Aberdeen might have been forgiven if they took us for the prosecutors rather than the defendants in a serious law-suit. Once inside the Great Hall of the Castle, each faction showed excessive politeness toward the other and the Court was clearly dismayed to find The Wolf so well represented. The King quickly dismissed the charges against Duncan. To do otherwise would have been to set passions aflame. The decision was made easier for him by his absence through illness or fear, of the chief pursuant, the deputy sheriff of Angus. His memory of that bloody fight at Gasklune, when the Isla ran red and his master was killed, may have persuaded him that it was unprofitable to prosecute Duncan Stewart. He was represented, unofficially as the King pointed out, by the two knights who had met Duncan's raiders and survived, Sir Patrick Gray and Sir David Lindsay, and by Lindsay's brother-in-law, the Laird of Fyvie, who was an influential figure in Aberdeen. But their intervention was disallowed. I watched the faces of these three men when they realised that their bid to seize Duncan Stewart legally had failed. I saw them conferring together, and saw also that they had been observed by the Wolf's Captain, Murdo McInnes. Something was afoot.

The Wolf calmly answered the remaining charges. He scornfully refused to accept the recommendation of Bishop Bur that he should rebuild the Cathedral of Elgin and his brother, the Earl of Fife, pled with him, unsuccessfully, to eschew adultery with Mariota Athyn. The proceedings were ended lamely by the King strongly exhorting his brother, "By good example and by good-living to mend the wrongs he had done to the Church and to his family."

That night, the Castle hall at Drum rang to the sound of laughter. Irvine and the Wolf between them had prepared a magnificent feast. The Royal party included Queen Isobel, the Princesses Margaret, Mary and Elizabeth with their Douglas husbands, and Archibald "Tyneman", the fifth Earl. The latter was a proud, arrogant man and conveyed by word and gesture to all, that he was set on a course towards the throne of Scotland. His attitude to the King was polite but patronising. By King Robert's side stood his brother, and his nephew John Stewart of Darnley, who later became my General in the French wars against England. He was an elegant man, and courteous to the ladies, who loved him for his good looks and his witty talk. He went out of his way that night to bring laughter to that mistrustful company, a task made no lighter by the Wolf. I had never seen him so animated and relaxed in manner, and I was soon to know why. This feast had been staged to enact his triumph over authority.

The banquet began with the cleaning of silverware and goblets and the interminable tasting of food and drink. All feared the anonymity of poison. The entertainment was lavish. A troupe of acrobats leaped into the air, dived through hoops of flaming parchment, and drew "ahs" of fearful surprise as they tumbled, blindfold, between outstretched swords. Suddenly there was a fanfare of trumpets and the Wolf appeared. He was clothed in the rich splendour of fur and wore a gold circlet of a prince of the Royal Blood. He advanced with slow, stately steps towards the King and Queen. On his arm, in shimmering emerald velvet with her long, flaxen hair brushed up into a plaited crown clasped above her forehead by a golden brooch, glided Mariota Athyn. There was an immediate hush. As they approached the Royal party, the King turned scarlet and Queen Isobel averted her gaze. The Wolf gave an elaborate bow. Mariota dropped a low, slow, curtsy, then, in her clear, Highland voice, she addressed the King.

"Sire. My husband and I welcome you and your Queen to our company. We wish only that you will have a night you will enjoy, and also that you will remember. Fear not to look on me Sire. I am no harlot, even if, as such, I am misrepresented by some. My sons Alexander and Duncan, aye and Walter and James, who sit amongst you, will, I am sure, persuade anyone who disagrees that they are mistaken,"

The Wolf laughed. "Well spoken Mariota," he said, and led his lady to her seat next to the King. His goblet crashed on the table. "Let the banquet commence," he commanded.

With the good wines and well-prepared food, conversation became free and lost its brittle quality. James Douglas of Balvenie, beginning to achieve the famous outline that earned for him the nickname of James the Gross, roared with laughter at a joke told against his kinsman Earl Archibald. The latter, concealing his irritation, replied with a sally at his tormentor, young Donald MacDonald of the Isles. Only two men in that company kept their own sombre counsel – Gray and Lindsay. They dissembled well, but a plot was hatching.

The Wolf's fist hit the table.

"Jester," he shouted. "The Play." At the end of the hall a door burst open, and the motley figure of the Hawk danced and leaped its way towards its master. Its face, lacking ears and nose, was painted white, and dark soot rings surrounded the eyes. The Jester's cap and bell whipped to and fro jingling as he capered. In the next period of breathless time, this strange creature enacted, in brazen parody, the proceedings of the day. We recognised the bellowing tone of Bishop Bur, the precise, clipped legal interjections of the Chief Justice, the throaty chuckle and quick answer of the Wolf, and the cajoling man-of-the-world approach of his older brother, Fife. The performance was so gently cruel, so blatantly insolent, and yet so funny, that the guests rolled in their seats and held their sides with laughter.

Finally with unmistakable clarity from the Hawk's lips came the King's high-pitched petulant voice.

"Come, come, Alexander, you really must be a good fellow and refrain from doing these naughty things."

The Hawk disappeared and a hush fell on the guests. All eyes were on the King. His face was ashen, his brows twisted in a scowl of anger. The Wolf, a smile on his lips, watched him like a cat. A chair was pushed back and John Stewart of Darnley was on his feet. Flagon raised, he addressed his host.

"My Lord Buchan," he began, clearly that all might hear. "If I am ever in a tight corner – and the same may apply to your Majesty – have the kindness to lend me your jester." Turning to the King he said, "Sire, you will confess that this Fool has mocked us all, in equal share, as is a Fool's privilege. We can take no offence, but must congratulate him on his humour and his skill. If there be some amongst our company who consider that the Jester had performed in doubtful taste, I ask them to look into their own hearts and say truthfully" – and he turned quite deliberately towards Patrick Gray and David Lindsay – "that they can see within themselves nothing more perfidious than the Jester's jibes. Arise my friends and toast our King. We wish your Majesty the health that has so far passed you by, and the continued allegiance of your large, bold but noble family." It was a fine speech, full of diplomacy and good humour, and worthy of the man who, thirty years later, was to be the Victor of Baugé the scourge of the English. It soothed the King's ruffled temper and the feasting and dancing continued until cock-crow.

Two days later, at dawn, Lady Mariota, together with the greater part of the Wolf's retinue, rode North and West into the safety of the gentle hills of Buchan. Murdo McInnes had not concealed from his master his suspicions of the Angus knights. The road home to Badenoch by the river Dee lay dangerously near the lands of Sir David Lindsay. If trouble was to be expected from that quarter the valley of the Feugh afforded an escape route for our assailants. It was the Wolf's way to strike first. Once he had arranged for his wife's safety, he rode with his sons and a few picked horsemen, lightly armed, straight through the territory of the enemy. Helped by Duncan's associates they were remounted in Glen Dye, high on Cairn o' Mount, and again in Glen Clova, with the tower of the Cortachy Castle in sight. As night mists hung greyly among the fir trees they forded the South Esk then the Prosen burn and were before Castle Airlie ere the guard could stumble to the battlements.

With a spear they nailed to dead Ogilvie's door the King's pardon of Duncan's raids. From its shaft fluttered the pennants of Badenoch and Buchan.

Eight

Young Andrew recovered. I longed to return to Plewlands and to my own family and had decided to tell the Wolf I wanted my freedom. But before I could do so something happened which gave a new and savage twist to my future. It was November, and the Earl and his sons were out culling the hinds. Lady Mariota sent for me, and I stood with her in her quiet beautiful room.

"I have brought you here Philip" – that was the first time she had ever used my Christian name – "to ask you for your advice and for your help. I will not beat about the bush. You know what a tyrant my husband can be and how his moods of ill temper have increased lately. You may not have noticed – because you have not known him as long as I – how his features have changed. He used to be a handsome man with fine, strong bones and a big head. But his face is pouched now. He never complains but I know he has much pain. There is something wrong with one of his feet; and have you seen his left hand – how pale and hairless it has become, how like a claw?" Some memory stirred. The face of a tutor sprang to mind, the one who had studied medicine in Montpellier and had taught us the rude but catchy aids to memory. Then it came to me. Standing in that room with Mariota I remembered the mnemonic.

A head like a lion whose face has decayed,
Feet without toes but hands like a maid,
Balls like a bullock though hard as a stone,
The impotent limps to a death all alone.

My face must have betrayed me.

"You have recognised the description?" she asked. "Do you think it fits?"

"My Lady," I said cautiously, "Such a contagion is rare. Has he been abroad in the last five years?"

"I am right then. Your face did give your thoughts away. Five and a half years ago he spent four months in Acre on a mission of mercy for his father, seeking the release of six Scottish knights held by the Turk. He could have taken the infection then. God knows he is a reasonably faithful husband to me, but he spent months abroad in that exotic place, the guest of the Emir and with all the women of the East to choose from."

"But he did not need to be unfaithful to you, Lady Mariota. Any human contact over a long period could produce this contagion."

"You are touchingly naïve, young Philip. But my husband would be in good company would he not? King Robert the Bruce was said to be a leper. "She sat down quickly, her slender body convulsed in sobs.

I waited. She was a strong woman, rich in character. No weaker woman could have lived with her wild husband and remained serene and in control.

"I am sorry," she said. "I don't often exhibit my heart in public."

"I am not your public," I replied. "I am your confessor or have you forgotten?" I was wondering just what it was that she wanted of me, how I could help her. She echoed my thoughts.

"Now you are puzzled to know why I have told my fears. I am in a dilemma. I love my husband, yet I am horrified by that awful disease. I know I could nurse him through anything except that. I have seen what leprosy does to a woman and I am afraid. I am afraid to go on living with him. I examine my pale skin every day of my life, searching for the tell-tale marks or the lumps which will deform me. So far, I have escaped. And yet, although I harbour all this secret fear, I cannot leave him. I love him," she ended simply, "bad tempered though he has become, impotent though he may become." She suddenly stiffened.

"Can you imagine what will become of us if that happened to him? His manhood gone and me still young – God." She buried her face in her hands and trembled from head to waist. "Oh! God."

I am seldom at a loss for words. But now, in the presence of this woman, her heart bared and her future life on the edge of desolation, I could think of not a single word that would comfort without offending. I stood an arm's length away from this beautiful racked creature, longing to take her in my arms, for I had no other comfort for her.

"I will pray for you," I muttered, and left her to utter loneliness. And pray I did. "Love suffereth long and is kind." I wondered if St. Paul had ever come across this catastrophe and what advice he would proffer. For advice he would surely give. He could never resist that temptation. I stayed on in the castle. I am tempted to say I remained in the hope of being of some help to her. In truth I was then not a little in love with Mariota Athyn.

In the weeks which followed that revealing interview, I saw much of her. And much too I did see, but never enough, of her chaperon, Hilda McDonnell. Whether by natural modesty or by fear of her husband's jealous rage, Mariota went nowhere, even in the Castle, without her maid. When the Wolf was off on one of his frequent trips to Buchan, Ruthven Castle or to his castle at Garth, Mariota would send her maid to my room with breakfast and a request to ride with her over the moors on a visit to Castle Grant or to Balvenie on the Fiddoch. She was a good horsewoman and looked well on her Arab, in a frock she called her Sherwood-green habit. Hilda rode well too and her style was natural. She hadn't the practised seat of her mistress but she had dash and a fine horse-control that derived from mastery and not from any careful wooing of the animal's responses. After a ride from the Croft at Auchtertipper her mare would be flecked with spit and sweat and wild-eyed like herself. I was first attracted to her, I suppose, by her fine looks, her high-spirited riding and by her controlled, provocative manner. She was a flirt and used the perilous trick that some women try. She would raise and lower the flag of surrender with dangerous disregard for passions and craving. When I look back on my desire for her it should have been plain to see that she was using me for her own purpose – or was it Murdo McInnes she was using – who is to know? Her grandmother had come to Lochindorb with the Earl of Atholl's lady, who fled there when her husband was killed by the Earl of March. Hilda's father, Matthew McDonnell, was born in the Castle. He was given the croft of Auchtertipper on the Duthil burn and was chief herdsman to the Wolf. Hilda was seven when her mother died in childbirth and she was left to look after her father. As she grew older, she grew prettier, and was chosen by Lady Mariota to be her maid but in the spring and summer during the herding she spent much of her time at the croft "doing" for Matthew. She had inherited from him the height, the freckled Irish complexion, and the temper. Once, returning from a stag hunt, I stopped at the croft to leave a haunch of venison. Hilda held my horse's head and gently but deliberately rubbed her breasts against my knee. "I'd like you better, priest, if you were a man," she said.

I called at her croft often after that, like a dog waiting for a bitch to go on heat. She teased, but was careful not to let my love-affair develop as I hoped it would; until one day late in September.

Lady Mariota had ridden to Balvenie Castle to stay with her friends, Jean and James Douglas. I enjoyed my visits there for Jean and James were about my own age. The over-bearing pride of family that made their kinsman The Black Douglas so arrogant forty years later was never obvious in them. Jean was as delicate as James was not. Scarcely had we arrived than Lady Mariota found that her gold waistband had gone. I have never seen a woman so upset by the loss of a trinket. Nothing would suffice but that Hilda and I should retrace our journey towards Lochindorb and search for it. This suited me well and Hilda gave me an interesting look. The search ended two miles up the Dullan water where the gold belt lay like a glittering snake in and half out of the burn we had forded as we came off the hill.

My luck began when Hilda saw it. She dropped down from her horse and lifted the beautiful thing up for me to see.

"I've found it. Look." She raised her excited girl's face asking me to

66

praise her good luck. Before her sparkling eyes had changed to guarded speculation, I was beside her by the burn and she was kicking and struggling in my arms as I carried her into the hazel grove.

"Now you are going to find the man inside the priest's clothing," I told her as I dodged her finger nails and pressed her twisting body among the hazel nuts and the blueberries. There was a sudden crash and a grey stallion snorted down at us.

"On your feet priest." The ugly face of Murdo McInnes glared from above. Hilda swiftly wriggled out from under me and stood panting, her eyes huge.

"Well, well McInnes," I sneered at him to cover my frustration, rage and embarrassment. "And what the hell are you doing here?"

"Can ye not guess, Hog!" He was out of the saddle and we stood facing each other like wolves at a carcass. And the "carcass" put her dainty foot in a stirrup, tossed her head, treated us to a giggly laugh and rode off down the burn. Murdo and I were stuck with our private war. The cause had carefully removed herself but our posturing remained. I was angry.

"What better time than now to settle with you! Come at me McInnes, bare-handed." And come at me he did. We fought and tripped, lashed out with boots and fists till the bracken and the whin were smashed flat and blood ran from our faces and our knuckles. In the end we lay down together by the burn all fight and hate knocked out of us and soaked our bruised, battered heads in the cool water. I can tell you I had my fill of Hilda McDonnell that September evening by the Dullan water – and so, I suspect had Murdo McInnes.

As with McInnes and Hilda McDonnell my relationship with others at Lochindorb changed. Even my dislike of the Wolf became softened by grudging respect. He was an expert hunter and the best horseman I had met. I would be commanded to travel in his retinue to distant properties, to wolf-hunts in the forests of Glenmore and before long I found myself included in the small group of men close enough to him to chide and chaff him in company. I took good advantage of this but often came off the worse. By his ribald and caustic remarks he could draw me and make me rise like a wagtail to a gnat. I told him one day what Bishop Bur had called him. He roared with laughter.

"By God! Old Sticky-Bur is more human than his sphinx face suggests. Fornicating reprobate! By Christ, the name fits, not only me but you as well, my lustful monk!"

Nine

A second bleak winter came and the snows lay all around us. The Loch froze and for a month we could ride our horses ashore over the ice. Then the crisp keen days of January changed to the mud and slush of March. Fires roared all day in the rooms, the windows were shuttered fast against the storms and whole weeks went by when no one dared cross the stormy Loch.

The Wolf, that cruel winter, retreated more and more into himself. Men went about with hushed voices. Mariota grew pale and tired and the boys became bad-tempered. I tried hard to seek his company, to speak to him on his own and, somehow, to reach this remote angry man. What I hoped for I cannot explain – perhaps some trend of conversation I could turn to his, and my advantage. He had taken to using the Chapel every so often but always the Hawk was with him.

"Believe it or not, Hog, before you came I often used this den when I was out hunting and returned late. Or when I had been drinking, I sometimes slept here so that Lady Mariota would not be disturbed."

"I felt sure you must have been in this room, Earl, otherwise why would this magnificent carving be hanging here?"

"You like my naked Christ? It is not the original. A fellow with an unpronounceable name carved that – oh! Some one hundred and fifty years ago, I expect. He made Christ a manly fellow. That's why I like it."

"What do you mean by manliness, Earl?" I asked. "This Christ is certainly virile!"

He laughed. "Yes, he's well built isn't he? Jesus Christ the meek and mild does not appeal to me. It strikes me he was a very brave man to stand up so well to his final persecution."

"To me," I said, "this beautiful carving makes it clear that we, all of us, have to suffer some form of crucifixion. That could be you or it could be me, Earl, up there. It may be that you and I shall yet undergo trial which could take us beyond our endurance."

He looked at me steadily for a moment. "Come Hawk, let's get in some target practice," he said and strode out of the room.

The outburst, the explosion, came in a quite unexpected form. It happened almost two years after my captivity and six months after my first conversation with Lady Mariota. The castle was full of visitors. All the family were present. Gilbert of Glencairnie was there with his daughter Mathilda and her sweetheart, John Grant the son of Sir Robert; Sir Robert too, for he and the Wolf had patched up their quarrel. Johanis de Brodie was another. Even the Earl of Moray, Thomas Dunbar with his mother Princess Marjory, the Wolf's sister, had been persuaded to come. She had been widowed two years before when Earl John Dunbar was killed in combat with the Earl Marshall of England at a tournament at Smithfield. The feud between the Bishop of Moray and the Wolf still smouldered, but since his excommunication and the burning of Elgin Cathedral, there had been less physical violence between the two factions. I think the young Earl of Moray had arrived on this evening especially to plead with him to become reconciled to the Church. There was talk about the exchange of land that was being proposed between Glencairnie and the Countess of Moray. By this deal Glencairnie was hoping to acquire Fochabers, with fishing rights on the Spey. Outwardly the company seemed relaxed, but I knew from experience that during these dinners each guest kept half an eye on the top table and on the Wolf. Tonight the more the flagons circulated the blacker became the Earl's demeanour. He had scarcely a word to say to his guests, but his bitter eyes seldom left his wife and flickered occasionally, balefully, on me.

Suddenly, he stood up, his fists smashing plates and goblets.

"Hog, Hog, Hog, on your feet you malignant swine. For nigh on two years you have wormed your way into my confidence, eaten my bread, drunk my wine, uttered prayers and your so-called blessings. And all this time you have been plotting against me. Mark, my friends this perfidious creature, this vile adder I have taken to my bosom. Prayers and blessings to his God be damned. Prayers to Baal and his unholy kind more likely. This monk, this so called chaplain is sworn to the Evil One."

The whole company was aghast. Baal worship was rife, although hidden, secret and feared as the very devil. He pointed a fist at my face.

"I suspected you when Andrew was ill. I suspected your witch's brew, your steaming broth. But I was prevailed upon by one I trusted to let you be. Aye, the one I had trusted for twenty-five years." He swung round on Lady Mariota.

"You, you deceiver. You, I have cosseted and pampered. Into your body I have poured my seed. From your body I have begot five sons. And what have you done to me you wicked, deceitful witch?"

There was a gasp of astonishment and a long keening cry from the boy James. A chair crashed and Sandy was on the floor facing the Wolf.

"Are you mad, father? What lies have you been fed? My mother a witch! Take that back, that foul accusation or by God I'll finish you now." This brought me to my feet. I knew that Sandy's fiery temper was only matched by his father's.

"My Lords, my Lords," I shouted, and Sandy turned on me, his face contorted with rage, his hand on the hilt of his dagger.

"Speak up then, you hell priest. I can believe it of you but what father has said of mother I can never believe."

"My Lord Alexander," I cried. "Don't act so rashly. Your mother and I have shared a great secret; perhaps that is why he accuses us, and perhaps we've been indiscreet in our meetings. We may have seemed to act like conspirators but believe me it was for the good of all."

"So," stormed the Earl, "You admit your secret meetings, your covens, your Baal worship. Woman – to your room."

71

Mariota rose, looked him straight in his eyes, turned and addressed me. "Do nothing, chaplain. Your life here is over. Pray for me." She curtsied to the Wolf and glided from the room.

"Before God, Hog, you'll pay for this," cried young James.

"My Lords," I replied, "I'm not to be challenged by you. Your father has misconstrued the acts and motives of your mother. I only hope I can persuade him otherwise." The old hate flashed back inside me. I felt rage twitch the roots of my hair and my voice was thickened by fury.

"If not then I shall throw down the gauntlet, and your father shall pick it up."

The fire went out of Sandy's anger. He grabbed his goblet of wine and shouted, "Fool, play us a song." But the party was over. Gloom and fear reeked through the room and all the jester's antics and foolery failed to dispel the malaise. I rose and stalked to the door.

"Hog," roared the Wolf, "I accept your challenge. We shall soon see if your foul pagan gods can help you."

To my surprise I was allowed to leave without hindrance but I spent a restless night. The Wolf's accusing voice kept breaking into my sleep and the events of that evening made a nightmare of my dreams.

When I awoke a change had taken place in my life in the Castle. The morning passed. No one came near me as I walked around the battlements and the looks I received from servants and soldiers were doubting, even frightened. I knew the reputation which the Wolf had stamped on me had stuck fast. By noon I was hungry and made my way to the kitchens. In these cramped cellars men sweated over huge stew pots, and cursed as burning fat spattered on them from grilling roasts. I was always welcome there, and as I entered the oven-hot room there was a shout from a solid fellow with a cropped head. Peter Grant, one of the two men rescued form the meat hooks of Castle Grant, wielded a cleaver over a side of beef.

As his chopper rose and flashed he shouted through the din, "Ho there monk, how's your Baal and cock this morning? You'll need all your cock to keep the Wolf away." He laughed loudly at his own joke and I remembered it was the custom of village people to nail a dead cock to their roofs at Beltane as protection from the God Baal. I laughed back at him, took hold of his cleaver and in mock fun he retreated beyond the chopping block. But as he ducked down he whispered urgently, "I'll meet you at dusk. I have something to tell you."

Big Walt the slaughterer appeared in his long, blood stained apron.

"Get out of here you tainted priest. I'll have no sorcerer fouling my kitchen."

"Whose kitchen you bloody slaughter-man?" roared Grant, "Take off your filthy apron and I'll show you whose kitchen this is. Get back amongst your stots and your hogs." Walt started to strip off and Peter laughed. "Leave the priest to me, Walter. I'll see he spits no spells at you."

Andrew and James were in the dining hall. They stood with their old nurse and showed no pleasure at my arrival. The nurse carried little Margaret, the boys' sister, in her arms and in her high-pitched voice she said, "You'll nae get ony denner here the day chaplain. The Folks are gian awa."

I went to the window and looked down into the Castle yard. Pack horses were loaded and the Earl and Lady Mariota sat on their mounts while the barge manoeuvred into position at the main gate. Andrew and James came to the window.

"Mother," cried Andrew, and the Countess turned and looked up at us. Her face was ivory, dark hollows lay under her eyes and tears glistened. She waved to them in silence.

"Where is she going?" I asked.

"Somewhere where you'll never find her, you wicked man," said the nurse.

James turned on me, his pale taut face contorted with pain and grief. "Curse you," he cried. "May I never forget how you have destroyed my mother. Hog, you deceitful villain, you have killed love. You will die for this. I swear."

The whip of hate cut me. Did I know then that in the nightmares of the future James's cry would pursue me, that his curse could stay with me until death?

I had started to climb the stairs to my room when a voice hissed from the tower door. I looked down. The Hawk stood hunched and grinning at me. "When the Wolf returns you are for 'The Ordeal'," he said. "You have three days to live."

I knew what The Ordeal was. Who doesn't in these times of black magic, witchcraft, and the secret worship of the old Gods? I recall, as a youngster, making the journey to Elgin, across the Loch, with some other lads, to see the "dooking" of Kirsty McCrae in the Order Pot outside the Pansport. She screamed for pity as she was twice cast into that dreadful water hole. She somehow managed to scramble out – her old clothes and baggy petticoats made her float – but she was thrown back into the Pot. She took a long time to drown and I remember joining in the excited shouts of "In with the witch, drown her, drown her." I had heard, too, of the witch of Auldearn and how she was rolled down the hill in an ale barrel five times before she died. And everyone knew of the burnings on Clunie Hill, by Forres.

As I lay in my room, fear haunted me from the shadows and my sweat turned sour. I was in this up to my neck. The Wolf's swift removal of Lady Mariota to some place a day's journey away, the attitude of the men of the Castle towards myself, and now the Hawk's warning, all indicated an unshaken course of action. The suddenness of Lady Mariota's departure unnerved me. I had hoped to talk to her and it almost seemed that the Wolf had planned to remove her before I could do so. I sat there and tried to find some explanation for the unexplained and, it came to me that the whole episode was too contrived. The Wolf had no cause to suspect his wife and myself of witchcraft just as he had no cause for any other suspicion. So why had he cast these extraordinary accusations at us unless they furnished the excuse to banish Mariota and to get rid of me. It was possible, of course, that he knew he was a leper. If it had become clear to him that he was doomed and the source of the gravest danger to his wife, would not his care for her have compelled him to force a separation? The risk of contagion between man and wife is very high. But would Mariota ever have consented to leave him? I already knew that answer. She was too proud and too much in love with him ever to walk away. I knew also that she was terrified of the disease. It seemed, therefore, that she might even have welcomed her husband's outburst and with it her banishment. How hard that acceptance would be I could imagine for she loved him and was deeply attached to her five boys and their sister Margaret. But the fear of contagion, disfigurement and the horrors of leprosy could be too much for her.

I wondered if the Wolf had guessed her thoughts. Did he then argue that she would never leave him – unless by such a ruse as this? The more I thought about it the more I was convinced that the Wolf had planned this extraordinary solution for it fitted in well with his own violent nature. It had to be convincing. It was, therefore, staged in the full glare of his public. And what is more, I was certain that my death would be essential to make the whole amazing plot ring true. There was really no other crime that could fit the bill so neatly. I supposed, for instance, that he might have accused us of adultery. But even if that accusation had been no invention, he could never have branded himself a cuckold. So it had to be witchcraft, and for me a slow and painful end.

Peter Grant slipped into my room at dusk. "You've got yoursel' into the maist unholy mess, priest."

His big friendly grin was what I needed, for the fortress of Lochindorb was a prison once more and my doom was reflected in everyone's eyes. I could trust Peter. We were bound, he and I, by that unique master to man friendship of the hunters of stag and the fishers of salmon.

"A rare wee place you've got here. Nae witchery aboot thon." He nodded to the wood carving. "My, but he was a weel made man!" He turned to me. "How aboot you and me getting oot o' this place? I'll show you just how the Hogeston-Grant disappearing act can be done. Ready?"

"I'm as ready as I'll ever be Peter."

"Right. Put on your black robe, slip off your shoes and follow me. Mind, not a word."

We glided barefoot across the yard and into the kitchens and a dark, bent shape moved silently ahead of us. Was it a shadow, a trick of the imagination, or the Hawk? At the far end of the kitchen against the Eastern wall of the Castle was a funnel-shaped hole in the floor. All the waste, offal and blood of the slaughter-house was swept up to this hole which ran straight down into the Loch. As in the water-pit, the water level came up the round well-like passage and the rubbish thrown in sank out of sight. The edge was slimy with blood and fat.

"Good feed for the fish," said Peter. "That's what gives them their fine taste." The hole was some three feet wide and gaped like an evil mouth on the kitchen floor. "I've had to clean this arsehole for five years," he said, "So now it's going to do something for me. It is ten feet deep and there's about five feet of water in it. It slopes down at an angle and is smooth the whole way. Where it ends there's nothing between the Castle and the bottom of the Loch but fifteen feet of water. We pack the offal into nets and weigh them down with cassies. All we've got to do is to hold on to a couple of heavy rocks, take a header in, and, so long as you dinna let go the stones, you canna help going right down wi' them."

I wondered whether death of Ordeal would be worse than diving into this hole.

"You're feart of the place?" Peter asked. "Ach we ca' it Auld Nick's Moo but it's nae so bad as you think. You can back out now if you like, no harm done, but I wouldna give much for your chances wi' the Wolf and his wild Highlanders. Och this looks like the mooth o' hell but I've been down it before for a bet wi' big Walt. It was a proper bastard but I took the money from the bragger which was worth it. Now, here's a stone for you and one for me."

He hauled a net across the flags with a boulder in its mesh. "Follow this and you'll end up on the bottom of the Loch twenty-five feet down. Don't let go until your ears crack or you could stick at the end of the well. I'll follow you down. When you get to the bottom let go the stone, kick up and you'll surface, if you're lucky, before your lungs burst. Wait for me. There's a couple of horses saddled for us in the wood."

I looked him in the eyes.

"See you outside then?"

Ten

I stripped off my cloak, hefted my weighted net and lowered it towards the gaping hole. I felt my heart pound slowly and strongly in my chest, stood quite still, breathed deeply and dived head-first into the tunnel. My left heel struck the edge of the hole, my arms reached the water and I slithered softly and speedily down the slope, pulled by the weight in the net. Down, down, down I went until my ears hurt and I felt my hands enter the ooze on the bottom. "Oh! Lord! Mud!" Panic gripped me. I let go, twisted myself round and started to swim upwards. My feet got a grip on something solid and I gave myself a push. My heart was pounding, my ears seemed sucked in towards the centre of my head. Suffocation screamed at me. God, would I ever reach the surface. Then when it seemed that I would never get there the dark grey sky of sunset was above me and breaths of sweet, sweet air were rushing into my starving lungs. Moments later, Peter bobbed up beside me and straight-away headed to the left. For a moment I thought he had taken the wrong direction, but far across the water the moon gleamed low over a hill and trees were silhouetted.

It was a long, hard swim and I had to drag myself across the stones and the final ten yards to the shore. We stood and pressed as much water as we could from our clothes then stumbled in amongst the trees. Big Walt sat on a stump, huddled under his woollens and watched us as we reached the small clearing.

"What took you so long? I'd begun to wish I had never got into this damned fool business." His voice was angry and edged with fear. "You know bloody well I'll be the first to be missed. When the cattle don't arrive at the Castle they'll want to know why. And they should have been there before dusk."

It was a cold night in early May. The day belonged to winter, one of these days before spring comes to the high hills, before the primroses or even the anemones are out. Sleet and rain sloshed fiercely across the moors. The sun had gone over Drynachan and the Loch behind us gleamed like polished lead in the pale glim that was left in the sky. A sudden hailstorm battered its way through the trees and balls of ice rattled down on the saddles of the three horses.

"Christ but it's cold," said Peter. "Let's get going or we'll freeze to death." We mounted up and took the South pass over the moors, through the mountain gap and on down towards the Spey valley and the Duthil Burn.

In less than half an hour we had stripped off our sodden clothes, and stood naked, steaming before the roaring fire in the croft at Auchtertipper. Hot milk laced with whisky fired our innards as we pulled on the coarse woollens of the Badenoch hill men. Hilda MacDonnell leant against the closed door with her arms folded and looked us over with amused interest. My wooing of her this far had been interesting but unsuccessful and now, as I stood completely exposed to her gaze, my bare bum steaming in the heat from the fire and my wee man the size of a mouse I didn't think my chances were improved. Matthew, her father, turned on her. "Get out of here you shameless woman, and let the lads get dressed in peace." She mocked us with laughter. Swinging her slim hips at us she slowly left the room.

"You'll spend the night here?" her father asked. I had known this matter would come up and was ready with my answer.

"No, Matthew, we will not. Three of us are missing from Lochindorb and it won't take them long to find out. I know that Murdo McInnes will waste no time at all in setting a war party after us. It will be as much as his life is worth if we are missing when the Wolf comes back." In the build up at Lochindorb in the early seventies Murdo McInnes had caught the Wolf's eye by his ruthlessness and determination and had been the Wolf's Captain of the Guard ever since. Although the Earl himself never missed an opportunity to go on forays, Murdo McInnes was the brain and the brawn behind most of the burning and pillaging. When the Wolf made up his mind about a course of action, Murdo McInnes planned it to success. The escape from the Castle of no less than three men would be a personal affront to his pride. I knew, adversaries that we had become in our rivalry over Hilda, that he would take every step to find us before the Wolf returned.

"No, Matthew," I repeated. "We have wasted enough time already. Thank you for your hospitality, but we must be away. If we are caught here you and Hilda will suffer the same fate as ourselves. Are you with us, Big Walt, or are you going to risk returning to the Castle?"

"Na, na," said the big man. "I've had enough o' yon. I'll try for luck and fortune elsewhere. I'm with you."

"And where exactly are we going?" asked Peter.

"Well I've been thinking about that and I reckon we should make for one of three places. We could make for Kildrummy or we could make for Auchindoun, but I think we'll make for Strathbogie. Kildrummy is too obvious and no doubt the Wolf and his spies are well aware of my relationship there. Auchindoun is too near, but Strathbogie is a place where we could hide safely. I'm a distant cousin of Francis Gordon, Earl of Huntly and Gordons are loyal to their kin. Mark you, Huntly is for the King. They always were Stewart men, but they're for their ain folk first. So we'll make for Strathbogie and take our chance with the Gordons."

The sleet had stopped when we left. We followed the river Dulnain and then the Spey and holed up for the night in a cave below Nethybridge. We were off at dawn, taking the hill path at Dirdhu to Tomintoul and by high noon we were far away on the braes of Glenlivet and down to the Cabrach, crossing the route that the Hammer of the Scots had taken when he moved North from Kildrummy to Elgin ninety years before. We kept The Buck well to the South and rested for the night in Clasindarroch forest to the North-west of Taponoth. In this same forest, Lulach, stepson of McBeth, had been killed by Malcolm, son of Duncan and the ghosts of the dead were all about us. It was an eerie place and the souls of the slain screamed at us in the voices of owls and woodcock and in the weird drumming of snipe. Strangely enough the biggest man with us, Big Walt himself, showed his fear most. This mountain of a man would gladly have taken on enormous odds against live adversaries, but the headless ghosts of Lulach and his warriors were too much for him. He spent a miserable night shivering under his saddle-cloth and was relieved when, at first light, we decided to be on the move. The rays of the morning sun were flashing at us over the flat summit of Taponoth with its ruined Pict fort as we descended into Strathbogie and by breakfast time we were hammering on the outer gates of the Castle of Huntly. We must have looked a queer lot in our rough grey woollens, bearded, dirty and hollow-eyed. After he had glared at us through the grill it was no wonder the sentry called out the guard. I announced myself, passed through the grill my grandfather, the Admiral's seal of office, which I always carried with me, and demanded to be taken to the Earl. He, a man in his fifties, welcomed us readily enough, but his wife, Sophia, who had come down in her dressing-gown to see what all the stir was about, greeted us with her usual frosty smile. I had met them both before. Bishop Bur entertained only from necessity, and to Francis Gordon and his wife, whose lands abutted the Bishop's at Fochabers, he paid court because it was prudent to do so. Francis was a King's man. His family has always stood for the Stewarts. Sophia, being a foreigner from Hungary, was inclined to view Scottish politics with distaste and suspicion. She was proud and arrogant and she saw in John Stewart, now Robert III, the weaknesses which were quite obvious to all but steadfastly refused to admit to his good points. She was much more sympathetic towards the Douglas cause and would embarrass the Bishop by extolling Archibald the Grim and Archibald Tyneman, the strong men of the South. For political reasons, therefore, she had no time for Alexander Stewart, King's brother though he was. And during my sojourn in Lochindorb I could see that no love was lost between herself and Mariota.

In two days and nights in the saddle I had come to the conclusion that I was not going to allow myself to be burnt out like a weed by the Wolf of Badenoch. I had formed a strong liking for Lady Mariota and I was determined to see how things were with her before I lived much longer. During my first day at Strathbogie, however, I saw that I could expect little help from the Earl or his wife. They could agree on nothing about the Earl of Buchan. It was plain that Francis had a liking for the Wolf almost amounting to respect, an attitude that would have shocked and enraged me two years before. Like many of his kind, he kept a mistress. She, however, knew her place. Her existence, recognised by Lady Sophia, disturbed the latter's equanimity very little and indeed the knowledge enhanced her position as top-lady and wife of the Earl. The Wolf had overstepped this convention and to Lady Sophia and her peers, his total rejection of his legal wife was a threat to them all. If he could do it, the others might! And so she hated the Wolf with a hot fierce hate and blackened his character with her shrew's tongue. Almost it seemed she took too much interest in his affairs. I knew that my concern for Lady Mariota would receive no sympathy from either Francis or Sophia, but I learned one thing. Both seemed certain that she would be found in King Edward Castle to the North. "And serve the beetch right," Lady Sophia had remarked. I passed my news on to Peter and Walt, who agreed that it was as likely a place as any of the Earl's castles in Buchan for Lady Mariota to be hidden. Peter seemed to know his way around and was ready to act as my guide. Big Walt, however, with a trace of embarrassment, told me he was not much good at rescuing damsels in distress and that he would prefer to stay in Strathbogie. He knew that the Earl was short of a slaughterer and he thought he could get the job.

"He is looking for that douce wee wifie and there's a good choice among the quines in Huntly," laughed Peter.

Lady Sophia's hostility had never wavered and I sensed a distinct relief in the Earl's manner when I announced that "my squire" and I would be leaving. I gave them to believe that I was making for Elgin without delay and to put anyone off the scent who might be interested I asked them if they would refrain from spreading the news of my whereabouts. By making a secret of our supposed destination and sharing it with Lady Sophia I was sure the news would spread quickly, and a false trail is a useful thing to have when hunted.

We left at dawn on a misty morning filled with the song of blackbirds and set off to the West up the river Deveron to the Haughs of Drumdelgie. No one had followed us, so we swiftly struck North through the forest of the Bin to re-cross the Deveron down river from Huntly. Leaving the valley and keeping to the heights we moved above Auchterless in the Ythan Valley, passing the old homes of the Picts on the Den Moss. The mist had remained low on the hill tops and covered our movements. We had avoided all inhabited places and felt sure we had arrived completely unobserved. Castle King Edward was a grim keep perched on a rocky ledge high above a burn. The approach was devoid of all cover but as we crossed towards the main gate there was no sign of life on the battlements. Scarcely had we knocked than the gate swung open and the Hawk stood before us.

"Welcome Master Hogeston and Master Grant," he said. "I have been expecting you. But where is the slaughter-man?"

Fear crawled up the back of my neck. "He left us on the way," I said.

We entered the grim keep of Castle King Edward and climbed the staircase to Mariota's rooms. Upstairs, the place was well furnished, well kept, pleasantly painted and carpeted. Her room was lit with windows that had views to the North-east down the valley of the burn towards the Deveron. To the North, where the sea breeze lifted the clouds, the Firth gleamed. Lady Mariota was seated, her hands busy with her sampler work.

"Well, Philip Hogeston and Peter Grant, I expected you to look for me, and I'm flattered that you've come so soon."

"Having been the cause of your banishment, my Lady, I could have done no less."

"Peter Grant," she said, "I think you would be better employed looking to the horses. I want to speak to the chaplain alone." The way she said chaplain made me look up sharply. There was an ironical twist in the manner of her speech that made me wonder what was to come next.

"Well," she said, "you see me safely housed here in surroundings more pleasant that you expected. I have my son Andrew, his tutor, my maid-in-waiting and, of course, the ubiquitous Hawk. There are no dragons to slay here, Sir Knight, or did you find it difficult to enter my prison?"

"Indeed I did not. I expected a trap and there is none. Why has your husband made it simple for me? And am I to be allowed to leave as easily as I entered?"

"You can go when you please, Philip. You were not impeded from leaving Lochindorb, were you?"

"Impeded!" I retorted. "I had the devil's own job to get out and was nearly drowned for my trouble."

"The gates were barred to you? You were pursued? No one would have stopped you, but you were expected to make a desperate break. It improves the story and makes your 'crime' all the more real to others."

I felt as I had many times when winded at wrestling. This slim, lovely woman, sitting with her hands clasped over her sampler work, her hair tied back in a tight bun and her neat ankles showing below her pearl-grey dress, had dealt me a body blow more bruising than any I had suffered at the hands of an opponent. I stood and stared at her for a long time.

She looked up and her grey eyes were twinkling with faint amusement. "It's true Philip Hogeston. You have been made use of and you may never know how useful you have been. I shall tell you now that I have always liked you and you have proved yourself to be an honourable friend, too honourable ever to betray my confidence.

My husband's accusation, your escape from Lochindorb, were all carefully prepared, as was this castle many weeks ago. He knew he was a leper, you see, and for Alexander Stewart, awareness always leads to action. He knew also that I loved him too much ever to leave him and he suspected my horror of disfiguration. So in front of our friends he proclaimed us conspirators in witchcraft from which there could be only one outcome, your death and my banishment. At the time I was amazed and as astounded as you were. I never believed my husband could be so devious, or that he had any delicate consideration for others, even for myself. I was astonished that he was able to keep up his pretence for so long and that he could even keep me ignorant of his intentions. The first thing we did when we arrived here was to make love. Yes, on that black bearskin he took me and told me he could never have borne to see our love destroyed by the nagging fear of illness. He knew and I knew that the only way to keep it alive and vital was to make it flourish in a state of partial banishment. Never fear, Alexander Stewart will make his way to my castle as often as he can. We shall no longer live together and thus, God willing, I may be spared his contagion. I am telling you all this, Philip Hogeston, because I trust you, and, strange as it may seem to you, he trusts you also. Your brief intrusion into his life has altered him in many ways. I hope it has altered you. You are very like each other. You are violent, you are direct, you are uncomplicated. Your belief in God is as strong as his. Your disappointment in the ways of God's Church is, I am almost sure, as deep as his. He took his own course of action. You are heretics, both of you, and although you are young you are the first heretical churchman he has ever met. I think he has seen in you some hope for the Church, something good and bright that will remove the need for the burnings of a future Wolf of Badenoch."

As she spoke she rose and moved in her graceful way to where I stood. She carried something in her hands. My mind was not on her but on what she was saying, and I only felt the pressure and heard a faint click as she fastened the amulet firmly around my right wrist. It was of gold, and embossed on it was the head of a wolf. "You have in your own curious way, Philip Hogeston, changed our fates, I believe for the better. Your heretical doubts, and your reforming zeal, although quite unchannelled as yet, impressed him. I hope there are more like you in the Church. If so God alone knows my husband might even repent his excesses."

I listened to her with amazement, concern and now with frank disbelief.

"The Wolf repent! God, madam you cannot know your husband."

"On the contrary, I know him better than any living person. As for you, Philip Hogeston, how can you pretend to know Alexander Stewart, if you do not even know yourself. Yes, you may bristle but I can assure you, you are still a lost soul. I think you have learned something by your incarceration, as you call it, in Lochindorb. Perhaps it was during the bitter, frosty winter of last year when the wind howled and snow was heaped high on the battlements that some warmth flew into your frozen heart from your companions, my boys, myself, from my husband even. You are changed, Philip Hogeston. You are in the process of finding your own soul. You will never again be the arrogant young priest you were when you arrived at Lochindorb trussed up like a turkey cock. You may yet make a good churchman but I doubt it. Look to your own safety whatever else you do, for my family is unforgiving. Beware the Stewarts Philip Hogeston. They blame you for a hurt so deep it will never heal. You have torn the family apart. That is what they believe and no one is going to change it, least of all the Wolf. For me, Sandy would have killed his father that night, or have been killed by him. But his cold intelligence will now reject me. I know my sons. Until my husband dies they will accept the fable he has so carefully woven because they can be told no other thing. The knowledge that he is a leper would taint us all and I would rather they thought ill of me than know the truth."

"And I, madam, am I to be forbidden to tell the truth?"

"Tell what you wish, my friend," she replied, hands motionless on her lap, her green eyes wide and serious. "Tell them the truth and see what will happen! You are free from Lochindorb but, until the Lord of Badenoch makes confession on his death-bed, you are not free from the Stewarts. Beware the young of the Wolf, Philip Hogeston. I know them well. Especially, I warn you, beware of James. He of all my sons will feed his hate."

My experience at Lochindorb had made me a more thoughtful man, perhaps even a more cunning, but it had certainly not made me a more humble one. I stood there like a schoolboy before a headmistress who was telling me that I was a scapegoat, that I had been made use of in the most wanton fashion and that my loyalty to her had been taken for granted. Her quiet tongue, like a skilful surgeon's knife, had pared me down to I know not what. My pride had been assaulted and I was angry. "Lady Mariota Athyn," I addressed her by her maiden name hoping to hurt her, "I fear no one in your family. You may tell your husband that I will not forgive his treatment of me and I hope my third attempt on his life may be successful. As for you, enjoy yourself in this prison as best you may, but never forget that I came to help you."

I inclined my head, turned on my heel and stalked out of the room. Reaching the courtyard I yelled for Peter Grant. He came stumbling from the kitchens, his mouth full of pastry.

"Can't we stay for a bite?"

"You've had your bite, now let's get going."

"Where to?"

"Home, your bloody idiot, home."

We pelted down the valley of the burn towards the Deveron, turned North at the river and took the bridle path to Banff.

"I'm sick and tired of being everyone's dogsbody. I want a damned good night in an alehouse."

A sharp glance came from Peter and his eyebrows shot up. "Ho, ho," he said quietly. "I'm with you there master."

We arrived in Banff at dusk, settled our horses and found the alehouse by the harbour. We were dirty, muddied and dishevelled and no one took the slightest notice as we entered. Like most alehouses it was a low-ceilinged, flag-stoned room with sand to cover the floor. A log fire blazed in the middle and the sparks and smoke curled among the rafters and escaped through a hole in the roof. In the smoke hung nets filled with legs of lamb, haunches of beef, sides of pork and huge yellow cheeses. Bunches of dust-covered herbs clustered along the shelves, rosemary and thyme and sage and bayleaf. Casks of ale were stacked along one wall and pewter mugs of all sizes swung on nails and hooks. The black mood was still on me. I had been curt and rude to Peter Grant. If he had given me half an excuse I would have fought him. The desire to hit something, to injure someone, was strong within me. "Where did you steal the pewter, landlord? You have a Prince's ransom here."

"You're right, sir, a Prince's ransom it is, but as for stealing, you're wrong there. The spoils of war, sir, that's what they are. My grandfather freed them from the English at Bannockburn. He fought with Adam Gordon and, between the two of them, they made a grand killing. Now what can I give you to cheer you up? You look like a man with two sore teeth. A quart of ale, sir?"

The first quart went down well and the second. The third quart dulled my antagonism towards the Wolf and his wife and, by the time I had passed them through me and into the gutter outside, my mind was on other things. The serving lass was short, buxom and big-bummed. She wiggled her arse at me every time she turned and bent low when serving to expose her paps. Peter had his eye on her friend. We ate well, drank more, and drunk, but far from incapable, oxtered our lassies upstairs to the bedrooms. I punished that girl and she loved every moment of it. The beer kept me in good trim, and I mounted her in every position I knew and a few more that she taught me. She wriggled and squealed and bit and laughed and finally when I gave it to her she nearly fainted with the pleasure of it. Flushed and exhausted she slipped from my bed in the dawn and I spent the next half hour thinking about her and catching the fleas she had left behind. I slept, then rising before anyone else was up, I walked through the morning mist and plunged naked into the white breakers of the Moray Firth. All coy and blushes, Betty appeared with my breakfast. I ate well, cleaned myself up and we were off as the sun broke through the mists of the morning, on the coast road to Cullen, Buckie, Fochabers, Elgin and home. Like a mountain adder I had sloughed off an old skin and was ready now to meet the world on my own terms.

Eleven

On my way from Banff I made up my mind to renounce my religious calling and follow my father's military career. This decision sustained me briefly in the first weeks of my return to Plewlands, but I found it hard to part with Bishop Bur. Clearly he and several others suspected that more than misguided zeal explained my two years of voluntary incarceration at Lochindorb. I had committed an unforgivable sin and given myself away by appearing at the side of the Wolf in the Church of St. Machiar at the King's Court in Aberdeen. As a priest I was finished, contaminated beyond hope of redemption and I found that my resignation from my religious calling was quite unnecessary. At my interrogation by the Black Friars a totally new charge was raised. Ridiculous as I found it, they were convinced that I was linked in a sinister way with the armed assault at the Bay of the Primroses. The theft of the Bishop's gold was far from forgotten. That I had killed a man in revenge for the slaughter of Chucker Bews was ignored and I was suspected as an accomplice. Nor was my defence of the Cathedral during its devastation reckoned in my favour. The fact that I alone had "ridden off" with the Wolf on that blazing night was "incontestable proof" that I was in league with him and branded me not only as a traitor but as a heretic. I realised almost too late the trap, carefully prepared over the years of my absence, was about to be sprung and that nothing short of my blood would satisfy the black brothers. Their greedy eyes were fixed on my golden amulet and my knowledge of its origin made any explanation a poor invention. I knew also that it was only a matter of time before the Wolf's accusing shout at that feast in Lochindorb became known to them. If they failed to nail me as a heretic they would certainly burn me for witchcraft. Secretly, and in fear for my very life, I presented myself at the local headquarters of the Knights of Saint John of Jerusalem, whom I knew had little truck and no communication with my companions at the Cathedral.⁶ I emphasised my educational accomplishments rather than my skill at arms in order to avoid attention and to my relief I was accepted for service abroad without much enthusiasm but, more important to me, without much scrutiny. Perhaps they thought I could argue the Turk into peaceful ways even if I could not kill him!

After only a month at Plewlands I was saying goodbye to my sisters and my mother once more.

"I do not seem able to keep a man at home," she complained, for her life with my father had been filled with sudden departures and joyful returnings. Peter Grant and I rode South through the mountains to avoid all towns and monasteries. So close had I come to the Black Brethren, their rack and thumbscrew, that I did not feel safe until I was across the river Tay and into the lands of Lothian. In Edinburgh we joined a new contingent of The Knights and sailed from Berwick to their island of Rhodes.

For five years I wore the blood-red cross on cape and shield and served The Order I think with credit. My best friend was Roland Huyton who joined in Bruges to escape the drudgery of his father's cloth business and arrived on the island in the same week as I. We were younger than most of the other recruits so that our escapades were in the main forgiven but when I look back at the first six months of military discipline I shudder at our indiscretions. We matured into competent soldiers and our superiors grew a few grey hairs. However, it took all of our youthful zest and high spirits to survive the Sixth Crusade. Few came back to Rhodes from Nicopolis. When reinforcements arrived on the island those of us who had lived to describe that disaster were given clear enough instructions to return to our native countries. The Order had no wish to prolong the memory of defeat. Some took their dismissal badly but Roland and I had had enough. Raiding for relics in Turkish-held Holy Land was one thing. It was quite another to serve a general we never saw and take orders in a language we could not understand. Our thirst for battle and glory had been quenched by the dregs of defeat.[7]

We disembarked at Marseilles and travelled North through France. Dark, cool forests gave place to vineyards and warm earth. Bullock carts, piled high with grapes, trundled towards a village. The fields were red and trampled and the trees were beginning to cast tawny leaves. A chateau reared itself beyond the town, battlements and towers jutting grey-green, above the lines of poplars. We were making for Eure where Roland had a brother-in-law. My squire met us at the trot. He had gone on ahead to look for an inn and appeared pleased with himself.

"Well, Peter," I said. "So you've viewed the 'scenery' and found it interesting?"

Peter Grant gave a grin that began in the roots of his curly hair and ended in the dimple of his cleft chin. "Yes, I've arranged my bed for the night, with warming pan."

"If she works at the chateau you'll need to mind your manners. Have you found out the name of the Castle?"

Peter pulled a face. "I have the manners of a grand seigneur when it suits me, master. The Castle is called Dreux and they are a frosty lot by all accounts."

At the name of Dreux my heart gave a sudden thump as if it had understood in some primitive way that Peter's reply was to alter the course of my life yet again. For a moment I could not understand why I had experienced such a flash of recognition. Where had I heard of the Castle of Dreux? And in an instant, fourteen years vanished like mist in the morning. In memory, I was back at Kildrummy in Mar. I was a laddie of twelve then, walking in the castle garden with my great-aunt Jean and listening with half an ear as the old lady, for the umpteenth time, recited the antecedents of my small but important self. There was a fox's den in the woods by the stream and I was itching to be off. "And so, Philip Hogeston, my little Oggie, the fine French princess, who was the second wife of King Alexander the Third of Scotland, was also your great, great, great, grandmother. Her name" – I knew the history by heart and remember, in my impatience to be gone, joining in at this stage - "Her name was Yolette de Dreux," we said in chorus. As I reined my horse in the valley of the Eure, like a once brilliant, now faded dream, these thoughts welled up to the brink of my memory and spilled over into the soft evening scene. The sun, low in the sky, cast long shadows from the poplars and drenched the distant walls and palisades of the Castle of Dreux. I felt my heart lurch again in my chest and, when I spoke, my voice was so strangely thickened that Roland shot me a quick glance.

"And why," said he, "this sudden interest in the noble seat of the Count of Dreux?"

Sunset came to the valley, the bold battlements of the Castle melted into the night sky and Roland and I rode toward Eure. William, his brother, was a slightly older version of Roland and a good deal plumper. He was a cheery character and, by his hospitality, was plainly doing well at his tanner's business. He owned a house on the outskirts of the town, a house of the old Roman pattern, with a clean stable and a well taught groom. I am fussy to whom I entrust my horse, a fine Arab stallion I took from Smyrna on one of our more successful raids. We had landed a small force and hoped to find and bring off with us holy relics of the Virgin Mary, who died at Ephesus. They got some old bones and I got Dogulu. I called him Dogulu after a famous Turkish corsair, and he had the mettle and intelligence of his namesake. I rubbed him down and saw him watered and fed before leaving him. He and I shared long and weary journeys and were in not a few tight corners. At the start of our acquaintance he had hated my guts because, accustomed to the harsh commands of Islam, he took badly to learning a new language. But our relationship improved and a fondness showed through his aristocratic arrogance. He was the best mount I ever had. I owed him my life, and much more than that.

I didn't mention my curiosity about the Chateau de Dreux until the next day and, by that time, I had learned something of interest from Peter Grant, who had been as surprised by my sudden interest in Dreux as had Roland. Early in the morning he had ridden up from his lodgings to squire me and, while boning my leatherwork said slyly, "There is a horny old Count at the Castle, you know, a lecherous old devil, so obsessed by his lack of male progeny that he ravishes every good looking dame that he can catch." Then I learned of the string of fine looking daughters procreated legitimately in his fruitless search for an heir, as well as his family of bastards populating the township.

"The poor man must be hard pressed to find dowries."

"Not a bit," said Peter, grinning. "He is as canny as a Scot. They are all so beautiful, these daughters, that the competition is keen. He has a system which weeds out the undesirables and narrows the contest to skill at arms." He told me of the tournaments that were held at the Castle of Dreux when any of the pretty daughters had come of age to marry.

At that time, forty years ago, the tournament was all the rage in Scotland and England and in France, and these trials of strength and skill attracted enthusiastic support and engendered sharp rivalry. These were the days of the knight errant, the travelling wrestler and the capering fools. The encumbrance of massive armour and even more massive horses had not yet reduced the spectacle to its lumbering idiocy of recent times. Nor was it so hidebound by tournament regulations and rules of conduct. Its fierce, fast battles had tremendous appeal and huge crowds used to turn up to witness them. A series of trials led up to the final clash of swords on armour, which not infrequently ended in the maiming or even the death of one or both of the contestants for there was a deadliness which later tournaments never possessed. This attitude towards combat is directly affected by war or peace. When life is spilling its blood in forays and in forts, tests of strength and skill seldom end in a victory on points.

Peter Grant had done his spying well. He and I have a close understanding. The master and man relationship is seldom obvious, but I know he would sell his life, although dearly, for me. I was set in my determination to visit the Chateau and Peter preceded us with my request, carrying with him the seal of office which had belonged to the French Admiral Bruce de Moray. The Admiral was my mother's father, a favourite ancestor for he had whipped the English pirates. The weather had changed overnight. Swift showers of rain spattered down on us and were blown East towards Paris. The floor of the shallow valley between Eure and Dreux rose perceptibly beyond the town and, in the distance, a tumbled range of low hills loomed moodily under a grey sky. The poplars were replaced by hillside of Scots fir and small red fields carried cabbages and artichokes. A few thatched crofts backed on to black woods, some only guarded by thin, mongrel dogs. The Chateau de Dreux appeared on our left over the trees. As we approached, the wood was felled and burnt to leave a desolation of tree stumps, each about four feet high, within a radius of two hundred yards from the castle moat. The charred stumps, iron hard, caught at the unwary horse and rider. The drawbridge was up and the helmets of armed men appeared on the battlements.

"They don't intend to be taken by surprise," said Roland.

"But by whom?" I retorted. "The nearest English garrison is at Le Havre and unless King Richard has changed his spots there can be no threat from that quarter." We crossed the drawbridge and awaited the raising of the massive portcullis.

So we entered the Castle of Dreux, a thorn in the English flesh for long enough and uncaptured through the hundred years of its tempestuous life. As we rode into the courtyard, commanded by the inner wall and the four corner towers, it was plain to see that the place was in a state of alert. We dismounted. Instantly we were confronted by the captain of the guard, who politely but with unmistakable seriousness and firmness requested to have the honour of our swords, our helmets and our short arms. This astounded us. We had never been received thus, except as emissaries to an enemy, but with six fully armed men pressing around us, it was politic to comply. Under escort, we climbed the clockwise spiral to the hall. The preconceived ideas I had about the master of the Château had to be quickly rearranged when the massive oak doors were thrown open by four soldiers. Peter Grant's description of the old roué of the Castle of Dreux certainly did not suit the squat, battle-fit man in his forties who rose to greet us. Clothed in brown leather and booted for horse, Charles de Dreux looked impressive. In all, there were some six men present in the hall, dressed alike in soft leather. And, in strange contrast, there were four female figures in the background, diaphanous in their satins and lace when the sunlight shone on them through the window high in the South wall. My eyes were fixed on the Master of Dreux, as he stood in front of us.

"Welcome, kinsman," he greeted me but although his voice was soft, his eyes told me I was far from as welcome as his tone suggested. I bowed and introduced Roland. With strict formality, he introduced us to the men present, and then, as if reluctantly, to the ladies, rapidly and in rather an offhand manner. Wine was poured and a speculative silence hung over everyone. The presence of the ladies had done nothing to calm my anger at our reception. It seemed that we were being regarded with as little friendship as outlandish captives at a Roman triumph.

"Has it become the manner in Normandy to display a stranger like an ape in a cage, or does my kinsman of Dreux feel threatened by two knights of St. John?" Looking back on my outburst I wonder we were not thrown instantly in the dungeons. I was angry and, with Roland in my company, deeply ashamed and resentful at our treatment. Charles de Dreux did not bat an eyelid.

"Cousin Philip," he said in his soft voice, "you have been long out of this country or you would be aware of the present situation. Our spies in England warn us that Richard is being pressed to send an army to regain his lost French territories. The English may have landed already and I have commanded that the rules of war shall now apply to this stronghold. It has never been taken and I will not risk one single man inside my walls whom I do not know and trust completely. You are affronted by our treatment of you. Perhaps now that you know the reason you will understand our conduct and forgive our caution. I assure you it is not our habit to fall short of excellence in our hospitality." I flushed, and Roland came to my help.

"Monsieur le Comte," he said and bowed elaborately. "Accept our assurances of good faith and out total commitment to your cause. Normandy's enemies are henceforth our enemies. Should the blow strike today you are assured of the support of our swords and armour. Forgive us for our ignorance in matters of state and accept us in friendship." The dangerous moment passed and we wined and recounted our histories, as was plainly expected. I noticed that the women had quietly joined us as we described the part we had played in the crusade, our opinion of the Turk as a soldier and our assessment of the chances of Christendom in the battle for the Holy places. We were entertained to dejouner and there the ladies, who had warmed to us quicker than the men, plied us with questions about the Turkish palaces and the dresses of the ladies of the harems and their appearance. The Countess, who had borne five girl children, looked almost as lovely as her daughters. Two were below the age of sixteen and I learnt about their married sisters. But my eyes were all for the oldest of the three unwed – Bridget. I was no novice in the appearance of women. I had met, flirted with and made love to many. But all the dark beauties of the orient, all the fair lassies of Moray and all the erotic charms of the Parisiennes were forgotten in the glowing radiance of this seventeen-year-old girl. She had eyes the colour of the northern sky on April mornings. Her face had skin so clear that the flush of her blood shone through like sunset. Her perfect head was crowned by a wealth of hair which, in the sunlight, glowed as polished bronze and hung like a cascade over her shoulders. She was gowned in green satin and, from the fall of the material, I could judge the excellence of her shape. Two gold bands of filigree encircled her wrists, and, at her neck, a cameo of transparent shell pink closed the valley between her breasts.

Roland and I must have passed muster, for in the afternoon we were bidden to join the Count in an inspection of the defences of the castle. Roland drew me aside when we stood alone for a brief moment as the guard was turned out. "I saw you lusting after that auburn charmer. Look out for your life, she has another admirer who will accept no rivalry." I had been so blinded by her beauty I had given no thought to this possibility.

"And who is that?" I asked.

"The boastful fellow with the black beard," said Roland.

Straight away I remembered a mocking laugh and a hooded glance and I smiled.

"I believe you Roland. I suspect I have a rival." The knowledge exhilarated me. Nothing is worth getting without striving and already I had determined to woo the fair Bridget. Six hours later I knew the strength of my opposition. We had dinner in the long hall with the crusie lamps smoking brightly on their brackets and reflecting dully on pewter jugs and the bronze dishes. Much wine had been drunk and conversation blossomed like a rose, and, when the ladies withdrew to bed, just occasionally the thorns pierced through. Roland and I enjoyed ourselves. We were in the company of horsemen and knowledgeable soldiers. Campaigns were discussed and old barrack-room ballads crooned or shouted. With the warmth of good wine in our bellies we told of our adventures with the Knights of St. John and of the disastrous end to the Sixth Crusade.

Our hosts listened well, but through all, I was aware of the smouldering gaze of André de Pacy. His comments were acid and his laughter brittle. We were stumbling along a corridor to our respective beds when it happened. Roland had gone on ahead and a single crusie lamp glowed on polished panels. A bare forearm caught me round the neck and a sharp knife found my ribs.

"Listen to me you Scotch braggart," whispered André. "Cast another covetous look at Bridget de Dreux and I'll not hesitate to stick you through."

I am an old campaigner skilled in unarmed fighting. I had been well taught in a hard school. As he whispered in my ear the training of four years wiped out all other thought. He was off-guard as I expected, for I had gone slack in his grip. Now in an explosion of power, I dived headlong to my left and swung my attacker off his feet and on to his back. I felt the knife slit my skin but my movement was away from his thrust and with a thud he hit the floor. I had his right wrist pinned and my knee across his throat before he knew what had hit him. "You will just have to take your chance then André my late friend." I put my whole weight on my knee against his neck and had the satisfaction of hearing his breath suddenly cut off. I sprang to my feet, seized the knife and kicked him at the same moment. Next morning, politely and in full view of my hosts, I returned his knife to him. He was looking pale, as well he might, and my remark did not help improve his complexion.

"Any time you lose your belongings come to me. I have an art at finding things. It must be the Scottish meanness."

That afternoon the Count arranged a tournament. He was much more perspicacious than I thought. I was, of course, now committed to staying on at Dreux, and Roland, when told about the incident in the corridor, would not leave without me. The Count dispatched a rider to Rouen, who returned to tell us that as yet no English fleet had been seen in the Channel. Messengers at arms were then sent to the various chateaux, abbeys and towns of Normandy, discreetly inviting their champions to attend the festival. The Count admitted that the occasion had a political motive. A conference of leaders would be arranged at the same time. And so on the last day of September 1397 the tournament at Dreux began with a fanfare of trumpets and a parade of competitors. Firstly came the fools dancing in their motley, the jugglers throwing their coloured balls in the air, the wrestlers flexing their muscles, the strong men tossing weights from hand to hand, and finally the knights and squires, on horseback and in full war panoply, visors up, lances fluttering their private flags. The horses were splendid, with fine embroidered linen trappings and pointed head protections, saddlery oiled and gleaming brown. It was a magnificent sight.

Roland and I performed with some credit in the sword and dagger contests. Roland finished with a gashed defensive arm but won in his division. By some coincidence André and I met in the close combat section. This time it was not in the dark but before almost the entire population of Dreux, Nonacourt and Verneuil. He was good, cunning and powerful. His feints were clever and within a minute he had drawn blood. Neither of us could overcome the other and the judge, probably quite fairly, awarded the contest to Andre. My squire, Peter Grant, thought I had been cheated of victory, and said so, but the Count was pleased. I could see now why this man was his champion but I was glad to note that Bridget showed none of her Father's pleasure. I had contrived to be with her often these past two weeks, and I was convinced that she had little real affection for the bearded Norman. We rode together in the Autumn mists, towards the distant hills and through the dark woods in daylight. I was aware of her presence in a crowded hall and longed for her in the hours of darkness. I believed too, that she shared these longings.

I did better at the wrestling. I remembered my tutor in Paris and his instructions – "Give when he expects to be taken and take him when he thinks he has won." André proved his greater skill at the Ring and I found myself second to him when the tally was called before the joust. Four of us were left in the running for the championship and, to my delight, Roland had lasted the pace. Our opponents were Jean de L'Eure, a veteran of thirty-five and André de Pacy. Roland and I were drawn first and he took two falls to my one. It was fated, of course, that Pacy should conquer de L'Eure.

As light began to fade in the West, and the dark forest drew nearer with night, de Pacy and I faced each other at the end of the lists. We had struck one blow apiece. De Pacy, to my surprise had unsaddled me easily on the first run. He feinted with his spear a split second before sticking me high on the neck. I returned the compliment on the next run and this was now the moment of victory or defeat. I withdrew my hand from its gauntlet and rubbed Dogulu's neck, crooning softly to him in a Turkish love song that always soothed him. I wanted the last ounce of strength and speed from Dogulu, and I knew he would do just what I wanted when I pulled the bridle. I raised my visor, saluted the Count and Countess and smiled at Bridget, and we rode at each other with everything at stake. I think my wide open helmet distracted de Pacy as I hoped it would. It afforded me clear sight of my charging opponent, whereas his vision was restricted by the slits of his visor and the lengthening curtain of dusk. As we thundered together I closed my thoughts to all but the patch of black shadow that would certainly appear for a split moment under his right shoulder as he straightened his arm to thrust the spear at my neck. Dogulu was magnificent. I felt his flesh between my knees tremble with excitement as he threw himself forward for the final shock. I turned his bit to the right and he responded instantly by breaking his pace and slewing ever so slightly towards the thundering horse of de Pacy. Too late my opponent realised what had happened. The tip of his sharp lance flew past my face and in the same instant the end of my spear struck him on the ridge of armour high in his right armpit. Dogulu's slewing motion shied his horse to the left and André de Pacy was hoisted from his saddle and struck the field with a resounding crash. I pulled Dogulu to a snorting halt, turned him and set the point of my lance against my opponent's neck.

"Admit defeat, de Pacy."

Slowly the fallen man's right fist came up above his head and he thumped the ground at my horse's feet. I replaced my spear in its long socket and trotted towards the pavilion. The Count glowered at me, but there was new respect on his face. The Countess was flushed with excitement. Bridget looked steadily into my eyes and the look told me all.

"Count Charles de Dreux." I spoke slowly and so that all around could hear. "I claim the reward of a victor ludorum. I claim the hand of the fair Lady Bridget." There was a murmur of surprised delight from the crowd. The Count's black eyebrows flared up and then his eyes smiled at me for the first time since we had met.

"Philip de Hogeston, my kinsman, I grant you your request if it is also the wish of Lady Bridget."

We were married in the Cathedral of Evreux, the lamp of the Seine Valley from Le Havre to Paris, and, although built more recently, so similar in appearance to the great Cathedral of Elgin, that I felt at once less far from home. Roland was at my side, solicitous towards me as always, and anxious to forestall all unpleasant moments for my sake and for Bridget's. The ceremony passed without incident, although I knew Roland was watching warily for any move from André de Pacy. I found a new respect for him. Honourably defeated, he accepted the situation like the noble knight he was.

The weeks following our wedding were full of joy and our nights together of undiscovered happiness. We visited many friends of the family and stayed in the Count's town house in Paris for several days. And at Dreux, we rode for miles and miles in the Autumn countryside. Gently fatigued by the fresh November air, our faces stung by the cold hill winds, we would retire early after a hot supper. And in bed with Bridget I discovered unimagined joys. I am an energetic man accustomed to physical alertness, but I had difficulty in matching my fiery Bridget. Her long smooth thighs encircled me from my knees to my neck and her smooth muscular abdomen pumped and squeezed the last drop of my giving into her slender body. And so the nights of our honeymoon passed in the hot excitement of lust and in the crusie light our twining limbs danced to the commanding song of love.

Our return to Plewlands was triumphant. The gean blossom was out in the Spey Valley and it gladdened my heart to see it again. My Godfather, Bishop William de Spynie, provided an escort for us from

Elgin to Spynie Palace and we embarked on the South shore of the Loch in the same ferry-boat I had known as a boy. My mother had taken charge, and its big brown square sail had been replaced by white canvas. On it was embroidered the Viking Ship of the Hogestons, the fleur-de-lis of France and the Triple daggers of the Count de Dreux. April sun sparkled on the blue-grey surface of the Loch. Willow catkins along the verge waved yellow pollen to the breeze and a flock of swans sang their way upwind towards the marshes. The long island waiting for us beyond the small cliffs of Ardivot stretched its length from Burghead to the river Lossie. Duffus Castle thrust stone bastions into the April sky and far to the West gleamed an ice-crest on Ben Wyvis. Bridget and I stood on the foredeck and feasted our eyes on sky, woods, and small fields pale green with the brierd of barley.

What a welcome we had at Plewlands! My mother, gracious but excited, hugged us both. My sisters were bursting with curiosity and the thrill of meeting their French sister-in-law. My friends, married and unmarried, came to welcome us. And honour upon joy, Great-Aunt Jean had made the journey from Kildrummy over the hills of the Cabrach to be there to greet us. Her sense of the fitness of things had compelled her to be one of the first to view the completion of a grand design. A circle within the family tree, traced so often by her in line from Yolette de Dreux, had now been drawn tight by my marriage to Bridget. Tears streamed from her old eyes as she enclosed my bride to her flat bosom and said, "Welcome my dear to your Scottish home."

I had warned Bridget whom she might meet but Great-Aunt Jean's presence was unexpected. Bridget rose to the occasion. Drawing on her own pride of family, she kissed the old lady on the cheek and said, "Darling Aunt Jean, I am really honoured that you have travelled so far to greet us. I look forward to visiting the famous Gordons of Kildrummy to return the great compliment you have paid us."

It was a neat speech and so plainly unrehearsed that Aunt Jean could only weep unashamedly and clasp her grand-niece more closely. At the age of seventy her cup over-flowed.

The new mistress of Plewlands was quickly accepted by my folk. Her charm and ease of manner soon overcame any initial prejudice against "The French woman". I was delighted to find her in fast friendship with my Godfather, William de Spynie, who had seldom descended from the realms of religious philosophy long enough to make my acquaintance. Nevertheless since he had occupied the Bishop's throne on the death of old Sticky-Bur, he had patiently suppressed the furore that my second swift disappearance from Plewlands had caused. In the years between he had somehow confused the scent and distracted the attention of those tireless bloodhounds the Black Friars. Because of the trouble I had caused we never became the best of friends, but Bridget won not only his heart but his respect which was even more difficult for him to give to a woman. She was made welcome by the guardian at the Castle. The Earl of Moray lived at Avoch across the Firth – and the old Castle, built by King David, was occupied by Simon Chisholm and Lady Margaret Chisholm. With the same apparent lack of effort she cast her charm on Matthew the fowler and Kirsty the cockle gatherer. Kirsty, her old legs swollen like tree trunks from fifty years of immersion in the cold, black mud of the Loch, lived in a wee thatched house near Duffus Castle at the Northern end of the Lang Steps. Gerald, her simple-minded son of forty, lived with her, acting as assistant to John the Greek, the head gardener at the Castle. Bridget had met the old woman one day when Gerald was home for his mid-day "piece". Seeing her son, Bridget said, "Blessings on you Mistress Kirsty." To which the old lady replied "Miss Kirsty if you please, Lady Bridget." And she added, with a sharp glance at Gerald, "I may not be married but I wisnae negleckit."

But of all my folk John the Greek was her favourite. At that time he was eighty years of age. He had been an old man when I was taken from Elgin eight years before and I had not expected to see him still alive. But there he was, the one-legged warrior, hirpling about the Castle gardens with his peg-leg and not a day older than when he had whipped it off and thrown it at me when he caught me stealing his prized jargonelles. I had only to meet him to be once more the lanky thirteen-year-old "Devil's spawn", as he used to shout at my retreating bottom.

Twelve

For some time after we arrived home, I was content to spend myself in improving the estate and in continuing my courtship of Bridget. A lot had to be done at Plewlands for since my father's death ten years before, the ditches had been neglected and my pastures were encroached by both loch and forest. I spent time, too, helping Bridget to make a home and Plewlands had to be adapted to her French ways.

"Jesu," she said, "it is little wonder you are tall and strong. How else could you have survived in this cold place!"

But, as time passed, a restlessness took hold of me. Questions I had begun to ask in Rhodes now demanded answers. I had heard a tale from a Scottish Knight about the Wolf of Badenoch which I found almost impossible to believe for he told me that the Wolf had craved forgiveness of Bishop Bur and asked to be reclaimed by the Church.[8] He told me that Bur had acceded to this request and had caused the Ban of Excommunication to be lifted only after insisting on the most debasing humiliation of his adversary in public and in the Church of the Blackfriars in Perth. It was hinted that half of the Wolf's fortune had been demanded in reparations. Said my informant, "So ended The Terror, with the Wolf of Badenoch, the antichrist, broken on the staff of Bishop Bur."

He was astounded by the reception his story got from me. Since my return I had enquired in Elgin and found that this extraordinary tale was apparently true. My questions remained and were answerable only by one man.

Eight years to the day after I had been trussed in a net at the door of the burning Cathedral and taken to the Wolf's lair on the back of a hill pony, Peter Grant and I rode to Lochindorb. I had last seen The Wolf six years before when he had branded me as a hireling of the Devil, and when young James had screamed at me the bitter curse that has worried me like a sheep-tick ever since. How would the Lord of Badenoch receive me now? We arrived in the early evening. During the long ride up the valleys of the Findhorn and the Dorbach I had remembered the painful events of that June so long ago. We stood in the clearing where Big Walt had met us after our desperate swim and looked out over a quicksilver loch to gaunt walls black against midsummer twilight. There was a boatman in a rough hut by the water's edge and we persuaded him by threats and bribes to carry a message across to his master. I was in no hurry to place myself again at the mercy of The Wolf, and reckoned that perhaps the safest way to enter his den was by invitation. Peter and I sheltered from the rain in the ferryman's small stinking bothy. We waited all that night, all the next day and night and when the boatman, Angus, returned we were steeling ourselves for yet another night on his foul bed of skins and flea-infested hay. He was truculent and blamed us for being thrown in the dungeon. He was also drunk which belied his story. The message from Alexander Stewart read:

"Since you have waited so long your motives may not be idle curiosity. Hell must be preferred to Angus' filth. I expect you at dusk."

I had hours to spare and we rode our horses up to the pass in the hills overlooking the Spey, and to the Croft at Auchtertipper.

"I want to see Murdo McInnes. Go and prepare the way."

"I doubt if you really want to see that black-faced villain," replied Peter. "But I widnae mind a peek at Hilda again, and nor wad you. I would like to ken if she has tamed him or the ither way round, since he took her to wife."

I returned, crossed the Loch and was led to the same small panelled room where, as his prisoner, I had stood angrily before the Wolf eight years before. He was seated, as then, on the huge, black oak chair with the lion's feet, cloaked in the same crimson and gold brocade.

"You dare to return to the scene of your imprisonment Hog?" were his first words to me. We were six feet apart. The scent of myrrh was heavy in the air, but behind it, a faint but unmistakable odour, the smell of putrefaction.

"Does your shoulder still pain you Earl Buchan?" I quoted the very first words I had addressed to him in this room so long ago. In reply, he shrugged off his cloak from his left side, and my eyes were drawn to a white withered forearm, and a claw hand. His voice held threat and menace.

"You will regret that day," he said. For a full minute I saw only his ugly useless claw and heard my heart thud slowly in its cage.

"Your aim was poor, priest, that night at the Lang Steps, or there would have been no roasting for Bishop Bur."

"And no need for the shameful scenes at Perth." The words were there before I could stop them.

"So. It is out then," murmured the Wolf. "I am grateful for your directness. Yes, had your eye been better or your hand steadier there would have been no need for Bur's grotesque parody of the Sacrament at the Blackfriar's Monastery."

I digested his words.

"Why was it necessary Wolf?" He seemed not to hear me. His eyes, still gripped on mine, remembered a scene far from his bleak Castle in Lochindorb.

"Old Sticky-Bur would have wallowed in his triumph – if I had let him!" He chuckled. "It was necessary to make my peace with God." He paused. His bearded chin rested on his chest. His words came quietly but with the impact of stones "chunking" into a deep pool. "Also it was necessary Hog to deprive these common temple-merchants of the victory they believed was in their grasping fists." A wand of bog-wood flared orange in the fire. He was on his feet, his long gaunt face and sunken, fierce eyes a breath's distance away. "That is what you came to learn Hog, as I knew you would, sooner or later. I was the only person of woman born in the long crowded hall who won, that day in Perth. They had taken me to their temple, to crow like cocks on a midden heap, to trample on the Wolf who had dared to cast down their golden idols. They left in fear Hog, and I, in peace. I care not if they distort the truth and lie to their people. They know in here" – and he thumped his broad chest with his good hand – "in here, Hog, they know I was right, that God was with me and that my Christ, my naked tortured Jesus Christ, used me, aye, as his broom, as his fiery cross. My real sin, Hog, is that I enjoyed it. And of that, my warrior-priest, I am as unrepentant as you." His voice had risen. A dark shape sprang from the shadows and in the glow of the fire I saw the Hawk's featureless face. "Go now Hog. Your quest is over. Make love to your beautiful Bridget de Dreux – ah! – Yes, I have followed your adventures with some enjoyment and I admit with some envy. – Hawk!" I felt rather than saw the nimble dwarf reach the door behind me. His small hand gripped my arm and I was led to the Watergate.

My horse took me swiftly up the hill path to the Croft at Auchtertipper but I remember nothing of the journey, so filled was my head with my meeting with the Wolf. Was he mad? How else could he have drawn satisfaction from the Blackfriar's debauchle? I had heard my churchmen friends describe it differently. Murdo McInnes had been by his side, as always, for part of the ceremony at Perth and if necessary, I would force the truth out of him.

Hilda opened the door to me. She was even more beautiful than in her maiden days. Was it for my benefit she wore her mistress's Sherwood-green habit? The scene among the hazel bushes by the Dullan Water flashed bright into the eye of my mind, and from the sudden blush and sly look, into Hilda's as well. "Ye're married then, monk," she mocked me. "And to a hot Frenchy piece by all accounts." Her husband stepped up, closed the door and handed me a mug of spirits.

"I'll not say I'm ower pleased tae see ye again Hog. Whit wis it Peter Grant said couldnae be telt to onyone but yersel?" There were to be no preliminaries. I felt Murdo's fist at my face six years past. I knew this man well.

"Tell me how Alexander Stewart, so-called Wolf of Badenoch, looked in sack-cloth at Bishop Bur's feet." Murdo's reaction was instant. The mug was smashed from my hand and his fingers were on my throat. Hilda screamed. Peter Grant leapt on Murdo's back, and the three of us crashed to the floor smashing a chair on the way down. I was on my feet, but not as quickly as Murdo and I would have been felled but for Hilda. Eyes ablaze, she crouched like a lioness, and in her right hand was a long knife. Her face was drained of all blood and she spat her words at the three of us.

"I'll knife the first to move, even if it be my own husband. Ye'll behave like men, not beasts, in my hoose." The breath left us in sighs and as we sat down together round the tough beech-wood table, tempers slowly cooled.

"I'll tell ye, ye bastard priest, how my master faced Bur in Perth. Nae doot ye've heard a' the lies yer Papish friends can foul him wi'. Now I give ye the truth." Murdo's dark ugly face creased into the nearest resemblance to a grin I had ever seen on it. "They were bloody scared, the hale lot of them. Even when he strode, slow-like, between a' that glitter and tinsel frae France and England, they never kenned if it was real or no, or if he held a spear beneath his wolf's pelt. Aye, sack-cloth be damned. His face was grey wi' ash-dust, but he wore a cloak of wolf-skins wi' the fur agin his naked flesh. New slain they were, wi' the blood drippin' af the fley marks on to the floor. I wish ye'd seen their faces under their golden mitres. The whole crew fell back when the Wolf appeared. Bishop Bur, gie him his due, was the only one that stood his ground. And these two fair glowered at each other. Aye, they called on him to debase hissel and he bowed low at the Bishop. But Bur's triumph was a wee bit spiled when the two wolf heads slobbered spit and blood a' ower his fine claes. A humiliation, they ca'ed it. Fa was humiliated? Nae the Wolf!"

Thirteen

The passionate early years of marriage are the best we ever knew and for me the dangerous times which followed saw the full bloom of youthful love. Lochindorb receded from my thoughts. The hurt to my conceit still rankled and the Curse of James Stewart sometimes troubled my dreams. But the excitement of battle and the joyful homecomings drove away such sombre thoughts – or drove them under cover. We lived in the twilight years before the dawn of Scotland's golden age, a twilight, which could have become darkness but for the defence of the realm by Archibald Tyneman Earl of Douglas. The friendship I had made at Lochindorb with Jean and James Douglas of Balvenie Castle and my father's good name as a soldier, both helped me to gain the acquaintance of Earl Archibald. The Duffus troop of horse rode with Douglas in battle with the Percies and later we were hurled against the invasion of the English King Henry IV. From concealment in the Pentland Hills we watched helplessly as Edinburgh burned, then harried the enemy's lines of supply and plundered his baggage train until with an empty belly he lumbered South beyond the Tweed. I fought again under Earl Archibald at the Battle of Homildon Hill and escaped the finality of Death or the ignominy of capture only by being thrown by my horse into uncomfortable hiding in a thicket of hawthorn. These sorties to the borders although infrequent were most rewarding. The capture of an English Army pay-chest brought a goodly share of the gold to Plewlands. Bridget and I had time in plenty to enjoy each other's company and wealth enough to improve the estate and provide for the education of our children.

John, conceived on our first visit to the Castle of Kildrummy, was born, of course, at Plewlands. Bridget was nearly nineteen. She had the unusual facility, my young Frenchwoman, which, had they known it, many of her Scots women friends must have envied, of controlling conception. So full is she of sensual vigour and sparkling life, that we could well have had a child every year. But she would choose that moment to suit our passions, our surroundings, and the occasion of our mating. John's beginnings explain to me his hot jealous nature and his impulsive kindness. These traits, matched by our second son David, engendered between them a fierce rivalry and an equally fierce protective concern for each other which spurred them to heights of endeavour, and contributed to their violent deaths. John was conceived in the second year of our marriage. Perhaps we had enjoyed freedom from the ties of child-raising too long. When we were newly wed, Bridget had told me she wanted to live every moment home-making in Scotland and that she would like to avoid starting a family for a year at least. This dismayed me quite a bit I can tell you, until she explained, in her twinkling way, that she would not necessarily have to lock me out. I was twenty-eight and a virile fellow. She had her way and I was happy to love her often and with abandon, cheerfully leaving the rest to her. Looking back now on the events at Kildrummy I realise that, as all pursuits are dull without danger, so, in lovemaking, that intensely enjoyable act becomes less satisfying when robbed of its real purpose. A little niggling doubt burrowed unto me, like a weavil in a biscuit. I had begun to wonder if we were not in a fool's paradise and that there might be no children in us at all.

Already at Kildrummy was the family of MacDonalds – Alan and Lena and their three fine sons. Alan was my own age, a son of that grand chieftain of the Western Isles, stocky, durable and bubbling over with life and laughter. Lena, three years older than Bridget, had the smooth, oval face, the silken hair and grey eyes of all beautiful Swedish women. They had met in Orkney where Alan was on a diplomatic mission to the Prince of Norway. Lena, the daughter of a rich Viking turned merchant in Kirkwall, had cast her spell on the young Westerner. Her father stoked his grizzled beard in approval and they were wed in St. Magnus Cathedral with the full pomp and pageantry that both we Gaels and the Norse folk so enjoy. Alan said the whole of Kirkwall was drunk for a week. The young couple sailed from Stromness to Kismul Castle in Barra on a long-ship loaned by Prince Olaf and streaming the banners of the Isles and of the court of Norway, and the blood-red burgee of Lena's Viking father. Alan's diplomatic mission had been supremely successful. We had this in common, he and I, that we had made good love-matches with girls from different cultures. But Alan had three sons. I had none.

Our last evening at Kildrummy followed a stag hunt which had drawn us far across the mountains to the valley of the Dee. The Kildrummy party was made up of Gordons, Hays, Stewarts, all expert riders and hunters. But it was Alan MacDonald who made the kill. The stag, for the second time, had been cornered by the hounds. It had broken free one hour before, killing a dog. Now it stood at bay at the far end of a small plateau approached by a knife-edged ridge and ending in a steep tumble of loose scree. The beast was a noble giant of fourteen points with a chest like a warhorse, and he stood there eyeing his adversaries, blowing and pawing at them as they circled and growled. Alan, John Gordon and I were first on the scene and, to our dismay, the stag burst through the baying hounds and vanished over the edge of the cliff. Our birse was up. We drove our mounts at reckless speed to the edge. The stag was not thirty yards below, plunging desperately to keep its feet on the moving scree. With a whoop and a yell Alan launched his horse from the precipice and landed haunch down on the sliding slope of dust and stones. The whole mountain was on the move as horse and stag plunged downwards towards the valley floor. We watched from above in horror as boulders, dislodged by the landslide, crashed, tumbled and bounded towards them. Somehow, stag and horse, with Alan riding as never before, kept ahead of and below the hissing mountain slope until they vanished from our view in a cloud of rising dust.

"God," said John Gordon, "I nivver thocht tae see onything like yon. The bloody madman!" But his tone carried respect. John, another of Aunt Jean's brood of grand-nephews, was the finest hunter in Strathdon. By a long detour we reached Alan. He was perched on the stag's rump, his face, arms and legs red with his own blood and that of the gralloched beast. His hunting spear stuck out from behind its left shoulder. "Christ," he said, "But thon was a rare chase. Going down that scree slope was like riding a sailor's whore in a gale at sea – and I can tell you that takes some doing."

I have never relished playing second fiddle. Alan was on top of his world. When he got back to the Castle a message awaited him advising that he had been selected as aide to our Ambassador at the French Court, a position I too had applied for and coveted. We had a farewell session in the Fortress Hall, and the insidious poison of envy spread from my thwarted ego to my thwarted balls. I quarrelled with Alan and since we were both more than drunk, the argument was stupid, insulting and, of course, quite unnecessary. I joined Bridget in our room in one of the massive corner-towers in a foul mood. Even the argument had gone badly for me. Drunk, angry and dispirited, I longed for the comfort and solace of her slender body. The air was warm. Soft summer scents of night-stock and lavender drifted up from the castle gardens. Bridget was asleep and her right shoulder and arm lay over the bedclothes, sheathed in fine lawn. A flush swept to the roots of my hair. I stretched out my hand and plucked off the sheet that covered her. She lay in a long nightdress. On a warm August night this was so unusual that I felt it like a slap across my face. She looked up from the pillow. "Philip," she said. "You should not have come to me tonight. I love you as I can love no other man, but while your heart is full of envy you can have no place in mine. I do not envy Lena her new Avignon home though I am a Frenchwoman and miss my country. I do not envy her her fine sons, for I know I can give you the children you need. Do not lust after my body tonight, my love. Rest well. We shall ride tomorrow into the sunrise and mate together under the elms and on the green mosses of the river bank." And, as dawn shot its pale fingers from beyond the Howe of Alford, we rode past the sleepy sentry, over the green fields, and South to the winding river. There, to the cooing of the wood-pigeons and the cries of the tumbling wollachies, in a fairyland of spangled web that sparkled like diamonds in the early sunshine, we conceived our first born.

Is it foolish to think that the hot act of conception instils an imperishable something to the character of the child? I look at Catherine with her bright auburn hair and her dancing sea-green eyes, and hear again the soft songs of the Island folk, the long, slow sough of the Atlantic rollers on a bright sandy beach and the crooning of grey seals on the skerries. I watch young Jean's lissom limbs as she dances the graceful Galliard or with sensuous abandon acts the courtesan in La Volta, and I remember the Gypsy Camp in the Forest of Dreux, the sad shrill cadence of an Eastern pipe, and, by the leaping light of a blazing fire, the explosive fury of the wild dances of Hungary. I feel again, in my inner self the welling joy of these matings and know with a sureness that, in each of these supreme moments of our life together our harmony has mingled with our love juices and in some incredible way spilled over into the new being we have created.

Life cannot be for ever filled with joy. Fate holds us in its scales and horror and despair were stacked against us. The year was 1411 when death came to my family on a Chariot of War. The stench of burning towns which hung over the troubled Border-lands had not yet polluted our Northern air. The horrid noise of feud and battle came to us beyond the Grampian only as a faint, far echo. But out of the blue of a midsummer sky the Blind Fury was in our midst. MacDonald, Lord of the Isles, drunk with ambition, his dreams fostered by secret treaty with the English King, swooped from the North. He was hungry for the lands of Ross, and, having conquered them, he now coveted the Kingdom. He faced the King's Army led by Alexander

Stewart, Earl of Mar, at Harlaw near Aberdeen. That bloody battle was a disastrous victory for Scotland and a total defeat for me and my family. For, to the deadly scene, against all instruction, rode my two fair and lovely boys, fearless as young hunters, and impatient to be men. Of that battle, until now, I have been unable to speak, so filled with horrifying memory was that day of carnage. Bridget who understands far better than I the conflicts that rage within me, has persuaded me to purge myself of these demons and to write a confession of the events.

Donald MacDonald, King of the Isles, had cut his way in a broad swathe through the Earldoms of Moray and Huntly and had quartered his huge army with their followers and booty in the lands of Strathbogie. The havoc of that advance was described to us at Plewlands by my cousin John Gordon, my mother's nephew from Kildrummy. Caught at Huntly Castle when the horde descended upon it, he rode for help to Moray and to Duffus Castle. He found the Earl far off in Easter Ross protecting his lands and properties there from the stragglers of MacDonald's army. There was little hope for us if MacDonald won so I set out for war with John Gordon, Peter Grant and my Duffus troop of twenty horsemen. The trail of the invading Islemen was half a mile wide and the piles of dung left by their horses and cattle, and the mess of their camp-sites made it easy to follow. They were moving toward Aberdeen by Insch and to outflank them we rode through the Foudland. We came upon the stragglers and the stolen herds at Pitcaple. Avoiding contact with their main army we rode North-east by Daviot and the Lochs of Harlaw and ran slap into the Army of the Earl of Mar as it forded the Ury at Conglas.

The sentry at the door of the General's tent ran his hands expertly over my arms, my waist and my legs from thighs to ankles. He was thorough and I knew what he sought. Satisfied, he lifted the heavy skin flaps, and I went in. The tent was brightly lit by two ship's lanterns hung from the cross-pole. It was built of skins and hung with pale camelhair rugs. As I entered I felt as well as saw the soft scarlet and green spread of a dragon-carpet which could only have come from the mountains on the edge of the world in the lands of Genghis Khan and Tamerlane. The Earl was seated among his captains. Their armour, gleaming dully, was stacked in a row on wooden staves. My eyes stung with the smell of oil. In the quick rush of air the lamps flickered and steadied. Twenty eyes turned on me and I saw only two, pale-blue under sandy brows, and above them, tight curly hair, not now the flaming red of youth, but rusted like chain mail. The aggressive jaw of his Viking ancestors jutted toward me just as it had twenty years before. His steady gaze held me in a careful appraisal. The Wheel of Time suddenly slipped. We were back in a sunlit room in the central tower of Lochindorb Castle and I stood facing him in my monk's cloak. His light blue eyes widened briefly and I knew that the Earl of Mar, Sandy Stewart, eldest son of the Wolf of Badenoch, had made that journey back with me.

"It is a long time priest. Welcome to Scotland's Army."

The brief flash of intimacy had passed and the pressing business of War occupied our thoughts. Stewart questioned me closely. I confirmed the reports of his scouts that the enemy was only two miles distant encamped on the long Western slopes of the Hill of Harlaw above the valley of the Ury burn. I was dismayed to find that Mar's Army, enlarged by the Provost and Burgesses and as many trained soldiers as Aberdeen could spare, still numbered less than one fifth of the estimated numbers in the Highland Host. The Earl was strong in armour. The Knights of Buchan, Aberdeen, the Mearns, Angus and Dundee took with them nigh on two thousand men and horse. But he lacked the numbers of MacDonald's Army. This I told the General and he sat listening with his captains around him.

"The strategy of the Highlander in battle has seldom changed," he said, "His courage bow-tight, he risks all in the first terrible charge." So, Alexander Stewart, Earl of Mar, Son of The Wolf, disposed his forces in two main units. The smaller consisted of strong squadrons of mounted men under the leadership of James Scrymgeour, Constable of Dundee and Standard Bearer of Scotland. Mar placed this heavily armed force in the van on the high ground as near to the crest of the hill and to the enemy as could be managed. The rest of his army remained in reserve and, as far as possible, in cover. I attached my squadron to the pennant of Sir Alexander Irvin of Drum on the right flank of Stewart's army.

There we sat that warm July afternoon. Gulls wheeled and cried by the lochs on our right. Peewits tumbled in the sky above. So still were we that a large brown hare lolloped across the field and sat cleaning his whiskers and scratching the fleas on his neck in the soft summer heat. We had not long to wait. MacDonald's scouts spied the Royal Standard of Scotland not three hundred yards from where their army lay, and saw the contemptible little force of Scrymgeour and Ogilvie. There was a sound of tramping feet as ten thousand Highlanders pressed forward. The very hill shook. Over the brow of Harlaw Hill half a mile in front of us they came like a swarm of bees. They stopped, I counted twenty-one clan standards each with its tight knot of two hundred men. Long rows of green trouse and small black targets were outlined against the slumbering mass of Ben-a-hee. And many more had yet to appear. From the distance, at first thin and eerie, then wild and blood-curdling, sounded the War-Pipe of the Gael. The wailing music increased in volume, and, slowly at first, then faster and faster, the Highland army rolled forward. The pipes broke into a rapid skirl and, with a roar, the enemy rushed headlong at the small steady forest of lances while a ragged flight of arrows whistled their way towards Ogilvie and Scrymgeour. As the first shouting ranks of clansmen drew close these lances were lowered and screams mingled with the yell of battle as Lowland steel drew Highland blood. With a loud clash of battleaxe on sword the opposing armies gripped each other in the grisly embrace of war.

The Highlanders recoiled before the ferocity of that repulse. Had Scrymgeour stood fast the outcome might have been otherwise. But elated by the sight of the wounded enemy reeling from his thrust he advanced his men into the horde. For a while the battle went his way. The hill of Harlaw flowed with Highland blood. Then came the shrill command of the Pipes and the huge army of Donald MacDonald, The King of the Isles, fell upon the little force of Angus. Scrymgeour vanished. His standard toppled to the ground. Horses, gralloched by short stabbing thrusts, screamed and died, and their riders crashed to the earth. Mar advanced the remainder of his army and it was then that the Chief of the Clan MacLean, Hector Rufus, came face to face with Alexander Irvine of Drum. Cutting, stabbing and thrusting, I rode my horse to his aid and at that desperate moment my heart lurched as fear seized me by the throat. Two young boys on small ponies were galloping towards the ranks of Hector and in that instant I knew their names.

"John! David!" I yelled.

"We are here to help you," called David.

Like a black crab on the seabed, the ranks of the MacLeans opened to the assault on the young men. Then the claws snapped shut and my boys were struggling, enclosed by the enemy. I spurred my charger into their midst and laid about me with all my strength. David was down. John, shrieking like a madman, forced his horse into the melee to save his brother. Both vanished under the press of the enemy. How long I fought I cannot recall. My horse was killed beneath me. I struggled to my feet and, like a windmill, cut my way into that tight knot of green plaid. I slashed and stabbed and slashed and stabbed until all around me the field was slimy with blood and littered with severed arms and heads. The MacLeans retreated and I saw beside me the broken bodies of my captain Irvine of Drum, Hector, Chief of the MacLeans, and my two boys. The hot smell of blood reeked like a foul ghost from the sodden earth and as long as the battle raged about me I stood like a guard-dog over the corpses of the slain.

As the bright sunset colours of that July evening drenched the gory scene in pink and silver, the opposing armies, bled almost white, leaned on each other like drunken men on the Field of Harlaw. I sat all night long surrounded by the carnage of battle and cradled my two dead sons in my arms. I thought of Bridget and of her horror when I spoke the news. Peter Grant and one or two of my Duffus men who had survived, though weary to the death, mounted a guard all night long. The scavengers were abroad. We could hear the clank of the dead being stripped of their armour, and the "caw" of the hoodie-crows drifting amongst the corpses. The sun rose on the Day of the Feast of St. James the Apostle. The Highland Army had melted from the hill and from the slopes of the Ben-a-hee came the sad sad notes of a Coronach and the crying of women for their dead.

The slaying of our two eldest sons nearly killed us too. I blamed myself, and still do, and Bridget used up all her courage to save my sanity. I knew also with the utter conviction which borders on madness that the Curse of James Stewart was working within me. Others of the family at Lochindorb I had met in the years between but never James. The Wolf was dead and I was surprised to find that part of me mourned him. Sandy had inherited. He was his father's son, and his adventures have become a legend in the North East. He kidnapped the widow of the Earl of Mar from her fortress at Kildrummy, then wooed her, married her and took possession of the rich territories of her late husband. He had thought it expedient after that to disappear for a time, and went a-pirating.[9] But the deed which made him both respectable and respected was the defeat he inflicted on Donald MacDonald of the Isles at the Red Harlaw. He was recalled from Paris to raise and lead the army and though outnumbered, gave Donald such a fight that our own terrible losses were almost forgotten. But not alas, by me. I met him again in France, in 1421 with the Scots army that turned the tide against the English at Baugé.[10] I was glad to be there, for the Castle of Dreux was under siege, and to be part of its relief force was a great thing for me. All men are superstitious in times of battle, and none more than the Scots. Our army fought alongside St. Joan of Arc and until the day I die I shall remember the inspiration which the sight of that tiny slip of a girl, in her shining suit of armour, gave to the soldiers of France and Scotland.

Alexander's brother Walter and I were on the same side in 1429 when we took arms for our own protection against the Western Horde at the time of the sack of Inverness. Walter was a good soldier and displayed all the fierce wild energies of his father. He was a terrible foe to the kilted clansmen.

Duncan, the bandit, had become respectable. He had met his match in Jean Menzies of Comrie Castle who had pursued him with her sparkling eyes and hearty laughter and made an honest man of him at last.

Young Andrew, the white-faced child I had watched struggling with Death, now prospered as Sir Andrew of Sandhaugh. Little Margaret was married to Robert, Earl of Sutherland and Lady Mariota had exchanged her solitary castle for Margaret's ménage of cuddly babies.

But of James I knew nothing. He had vanished from the North. Of the five sons I thought him by nature closest to The Wolf and as proud and unbending. I supposed that his father's exhibition of weakness – as he would consider it - was more than he could stomach.

Fourteen

In the months that followed the Red Harlaw our greatest friend, the pillar that supported both Bridget and me, was Farquhar Beaton. I know of no man more closely matched in purpose and accomplishment to St. Luke The Blessed Physician. Many years after our first dependence on him, Bridget and I rode along the clifftops towards Stotfield. He joined us on the crest of the hill, just before the rough track plunged to the sea at Causea. It was a blustery early morning in June and great splashes of light moved across the countryside. To the landward of the sand dunes whin blossom sucked in the sun and glowed like an amber yellow sea. Farquhar led us to his cave and prepared a breakfast of fresh caught mackerel and plovers' eggs. He made good use of herbs, and the pink and the pale blue of the poached eggs lay in beds of nettle-green sauce. His grandfather, the seventh son of a seventh son, had been herbalist and healer to the Mormair of Ross and Farquhar himself had inherited his skill. As a youngster of twelve he had a way with animals, and by the time he was eighteen his talent as a bonesetter had spread beyond The Black Isle where he lived. He had set the wrist bones of an old aunt of the Earl of Moray when she had fallen at his Castle at Avoch. Farquhar explained his success with her, "The auld hen was as fu as a kite and I had a rare crunching and waggling at her wrist, which, mercifully, she remembered nothing about." She became a staunch supporter of his, and the Earl, much impressed, sent him to study at Balliol College, Oxford. He gave him a letter of introduction to an eminent man who had achieved respect as a physician when the Black Death struck that town in 1361. His pupil's quiet perseverance and gentleness of address had pleased the master and he learned well. Farquhar was a humble man, even at the peak of his fame when he was personal physician to young Prince James during the latter's captivity at the Court of the King of England and he travelled North with us when the King came into his own. Now a very old man, he lived the simple useful life of a hermit in St. Gerardine's Caves at Causea.

Bridget had consulted him four years before because of a hard lump the size of a sparrow's egg in her left breast. He had run his fine-boned hands over both her breasts, pressing his fingers high into her oxters.

"This lump will get bigger," he said, "and is dangerous to you."

Bridget had bravely submitted to the most painful treatment. Week by week Farquhar had inserted needle-sharp slivers of hard oak through her skin around the lump. These he had dipped in a herbal brew which smelt strongly of purple toadstool. When the inflammation had gone, weeks later, the lump was smaller. He had asked to see Bridget twice in every year and this was the sixth time I had ridden with her on this errand. The old man made her sit on a smooth rock, with her breasts bared to the sunlight. He studied her carefully and gently probed with his fingers. The twelve little scars showed white against the suntan of her bosom but of the lump there was hardly a sign.

"I am pleased," he said. Three small words, but the leaden weight which had lain on my heart for four long years miraculously lightened as he spoke them. Life without Bridget was unthinkable. Yet for four years the unthinkable had nagged my mind. Farquhar had warned me when he examined the lump in her breast for the first time that it was the seed of death. And now, that shadow had passed. Could it be that the Curse of James Stewart had lost its power?

Bridget and I rode out into the west wind, along the cliff path, past the war towers of the Picts, then, turning South towards the Loch we moved into yellow-green shade as the track took us through the old oak forest of Duffus, and towards the ancient carved Cross of the Kirk of Ogstoun.[11] Long-tailed tits flitted from branch to branch scolding us in their high-pitched voices. I dismounted in a glade, deep in the wood, and lifted Bridget from the saddle. Her eyes twinkled roguishly at me.

"So you are still jealous of the old man," she said.

"I am jealous of any man who would dare eye you as Farquhar does. You know he is the only man I would ever allow to touch your breasts and even when I watch him, old as he is, it is almost as much as I can bear." We were lying together amongst the wood sorrel and the anemones. A red squirrel peeped at us around the trunk of an oak, flashed its tawny tail and vanished into the leafy ceiling above us. The sweet enchantment of our growing pleasure bloomed inside us until she whispered in my ear.

"Come into me, Philip, now."

Fifteen

July 1st, 1439

B ridget has this manuscript on her lap, and looks at me across the room. "I begin to understand you even better," says she. "I knew that what had happened to you at Lochindorb had altered you in a most profound way. Whatever ill The Wolf may have done to you, or you thought he had done to you, you certainly came home much more the man I married than the conceited youth you must have been. I don't think you need to be quite so graphic in your descriptions of your lusty moments. I know exactly how Betty of Banff must have felt and I suppose I have to thank her for some of those habits you have in bed. You must stop worrying about James Stewart and his Curse. Lochindorb was a long time ago, and James was only a boy."

It is a hazy afternoon in July. Bridget and I are together in the tower room at Plewlands. Even in summer we reduce the house to its smallest possible extent in order to keep warm. The hall is never used and, unless we have guests, the stairways leading to the upper rooms are always closed off. We find the tower just right for us. On a windless day we can open up the large windows, and stand out on the balcony. From it we look over the tops of the trees to the battlements of the Castle of Duffus, and beyond, to a tiny part of the Loch of Spynie. In the South are the low green hills of Moray and farther away the long conical peak of Ben Rinnes shimmers in the sunshine. On a particularly clear day another cone shows itself to the left. Far, far over the hills juts the Buck of the Cabrach, near where Big Walt spent a night of terror surrounded by the headless wraiths of Lulach's warriors. Two years have passed since I started to write this story. I am a slow writer and I have had much to do in these days. Since King James's murder I have become drawn into the cloak and dagger of intrigue which has grown around his Queen. Queen Joan and Bridget have been friends for years and King James confided in me a lot.[12] I should feel flattered now to have my Queen rely so much on my judgement. She is surrounded by advisors but there are few of them to advise her without prejudice. As I had feared, Scotland had disintegrated into feuding factions and the Queen, hugging the newly crowned boy King to her bosom, flies from palace to palace to escape the attentions of her so called friends.

A cry for help has arrived from the South which I cannot ignore although Bridget hates and detests these long journeys when I have to leave her for weeks on end. The kingdom is lawless and infested with beggars who have banded themselves together into clans of brigands. The route is hazardous and I have to take from Plewlands men who should be engaged in looking after the property. Nevertheless, Bridget knows and I know that I will have to go.

The Queen's summons arrived with John Winchester. Bishop John succeeded William de Spynie as Bishop of Moray but we have been close friends since the victorious years in France when our Scottish army threw the English back to the Channel ports. When King James the First of Scotland was ransomed by his people from captivity in England, John Winchester, Farquhar Beaton and I accompanied the royal party on their journey North and only a year before he was murdered, the King visited us in Elgin, after John Winchester had been placed on the Bishop's throne. So when Bishop John himself arrived by boat from Spynie with Queen Joan's letter it was clear that its content was highly confidential and extremely urgent. One paragraph was addressed to me.

"For God's sake come to me," she wrote. "This James Stewart is a hard man and his motives are not the usual ones." Before I could fathom what she meant I experienced a strange fusion of thought. I remembered a dream I had a night or two before. A nightmare it had been, for I awoke that June morning soaked in cold sweat with my heart thudding in my chest. I had dreamed of the blackness of Death and the bright crimson of blood. And now the name of James Stewart had brought this hideous apparition back to the eye of my mind. In my dream, there was the sough of wind high in a black forest, the splatter of hailstones on blood-stained earth and the solid silence of water in spate. There was a corpse in full armour, Death's Head gaping from his helm, and a sword quivering in a rotted tree trunk, with a severed hand gripping to the hilt. Fast on this nightmarish picture flashed the scene in Lady Mariota's room at Lochindorb and young James Stewart turning on me, eyes filled with tears and hate, as his mother rode for ever from her Castle and from his life.

I read the Queen's letter and passed it to Bridget. I spoke sombrely to Bishop Winchester. "Well John, the Queen has certainly got herself mixed up in a strange company. She has been clever enough until now to play Crichton against Livingston and yet retain the upper hand. Tell me what you know of this James Stewart, the Black Knight of Lorn. She writes from Dunstaffnage and gives me the impression, though she doesn't say it in so many words, that she feels herself in grave danger. Is she prisoner of the Black Knight?"

Bishop John Winchester strode into the centre of the room. He is a small tough man who takes long strides on his short legs as if convincing himself and others that his lack of height is of no consequence. "My construction exactly," he said. He had the habit of staccato speech which forces attention. "Somerled, First Lord of the Isles, captured Dunollie Castle in 1150 and gave it to Dougall his son. His descendants were Lords of Lorn until Ewen MacDougall, Fifth of Lorn failed to produce an heir. The Lordship of Lorn therefore passed to his oldest daughter's husband Robert Stewart, who exchanged it for his older brother's property at Durrisdeer. Thus John Stewart his brother, became Lord of Lorn. That was fifty years ago. The Black Knight, James, is his third son, an extravagant fellow, skilled at arms, unmarried, and very fashionable with the ladies."

I was glad that John Winchester had finally answered the question. Like my Aunt Jean, his genealogy is never wrong but often tedious. This James Stewart was plainly not the James Stewart I had known at Lochindorb.

Bridget had been sitting apart quietly reading through Queen Joan's letter. She suddenly looked at us, eyes bright. "I am quite certain," she said, "that Joan is in love with him."

"In love with whom?" I asked.

"With James Stewart the Black Knight of Lorn."

The Bishop looked at her curiously. "You read that between the lines then, Bridget?" he asked.

Before she could reply I burst in, "But it's preposterous. The whole tone of the letter indicates the reverse. I would say that Joan has fixed one of her famous hates on the man. She had them before and the best I can do is to try to make her see that all is not black or white. This is the time of the Douglases. It's their power we must seek to curb. The Black Knight of Lorn is small fry."

"Queen Joan doesn't think him small fry," said the Bishop, "Her whole letter is full of him."

"And shouldn't it be," interposed Bridget, "If she is in love?"

John Winchester looked at us both. "Do you know, a woman's intuition is a remarkable thing. I'd trust a woman to see into the mind of another, Philip. We are moving in regions here where we men are babes in arms."

"I know I can't dissuade you from going," said Bridget to me, "But bear my construction of Joan's letter in mind and remember, it's dangerous to stand between a dog and his bone or a bear and her mate."

We are a brave little band that journey South. I am proud of my men – Jimmy the Gordon, who keeps bees at the Castle, Percy the Fowler, John Sime the Smith's son and seven others. All have volunteered to come with me, and have turned out like the soldiers they are. They could do no less under the stern eye of my old friend and squire Peter Grant. Catherine my oldest daughter came across by boat from Elgin with her husband, little Jamie and baby Bridie to say good-bye. I will spend one night at least with Jean my youngest, in Perth. I hope my remaining son, Alastair, will meet me in Stirling. He is an astute follower of Scottish politics, and will advise me on the most recent events.

"Before I leave I will go to Bridget. No doubt she will dispel the chill of melancholy and doubt which has come over me at the thought of leaving her. I must be getting old."

Sixteen

It was six weeks since Sandy Dunbar and I had carried Bishop John Winchester's reliquary to Pitgaveny House. In that time I had become totally absorbed in another man's life. Philip Hogeston had written his story five hundred and thirty-six years ago, and piecing it together was like turning a telescope on the man. I knew him better than I would ever know anyone. But the narrative had ended. Search as I did I could find nothing else among the mass of parchment laid out on the long table that was written in the now familiar hand. I had felt so sure that I would come across a continuation of the story. I couldn't accept that John Winchester would have stored a broken, incomplete history in his secret chest. I felt cheated, and leaned idly against the stone fireplace watching the others as they sorted and filed the ancient scrolls. The expert from Edinburgh was bending over a small heap of paper. He was a St. Andrews man, a teacher turned antiquary. We had met before on the rugby field, and he had played for Highland one memorable afternoon in the Cooper Park in Elgin when we wrested the Brin Cup from them. John Hamilton was greyer than I was, and looked the part of the dusty booklover in his plain half-glasses. But he still had the neat economy of movement which had made him the finest "stand-off" in the Highland League. I remembered his "Eskimo Nell" in the Tower Hotel that famous night.

So there I stood leaning against the Lairdie's carved stone fire-place in the house that had lasted since MacBeth murdered Duncan. Behind me, on the mantelpiece, in its small black satin box sat the dead Laird's prized possession, the skull of the German East-African soldier with its neat round bullet hole. My thoughts were of Philip Hogeston and his macabre dream. The hall slowly grew bigger. Bushes, heavy with leaf grew where the trophies of dead animals had grinned down from their wooden mounts. And two men appeared. The one nearer to me sat easily on a dappled mare, ears twitching as rain tickled the soft inside hairs. Her rump was covered in stiff linen and emblazoned with a Viking's ship. The rider's leather garb was wet but shone dully with oil and rubbing and a light, steel cap enclosed his head and ears. Iron-grey hair curled at his right temple. I knew him. I knew him as a boy on the cliffs of Causea. I knew him as a young priest wrestling with his soul in an island dungeon. I knew him in France, the lover and husband of Bridget de Deux.

The swollen waters of a river menaced the silence and Hate flowed like that tawny flood.

Twenty paces from Philip Hogeston stood a black horse and a black horseman. His mailed hand rested on a black sword. Black eyes glinted behind the broad slit of a black visor.

At that moment I was not certain of him. Then he shrugged the heavy shield and a red lion rampant on azure and argent slashed by the Bar Sinister shouted his identity.

The vision passed. John Hamilton, sitting at his work, watched me with a strange enquiring expression. In his matter of fact way he said,

"You've lost something Mac? Well, I've found it. With the Bishop's compliments." I moved across to where he sat and carefully lifted the small crumpled paper pile. I knew then, without a doubt, that I held in my hands the last chapter in the life of Philip Hogeston.....

Seventeen

The Story that Peter Grant told to Bishop John Winchester and Lady Bridget Hogeston

Sir Philip Hogeston and ten good men from Duffus, with myself as their Lieutenant, set out from Plewlands on July the tenth, 1439. We crossed the Cabrach Hills to Kildrummy and thence by the Mearns to Strathmore and Perth, where we lodged with Lady Jean, Sir Philip's younger daughter.

At Stirling the master spoke with Livingston of Callander, who told him that Queen Joan and her children were the prisoners of Sir James Stewart, The Black Knight of Lorn, at Dunstaffnage Castle. He seemed most anxious to rescue her and the Royal children, and was clearly greatly relived to have Sir Philip and ourselves to help him. It was finally agreed that our small force would journey by the Pass of Brander to Lorn, seek peaceful terms for the return of Queen Joan and her children, and convey them back to Stirling Castle. I never trusted Livingston and I warned Sir Philip that I suspected double-dealing. It was a pity we did not stop in Stirling until Master Alastair arrived from Edinburgh. His advice was always sound and without a doubt he would have known of the relations between the Queen and Livingston. Sir Philip had decided to wait Alastair's arrival, but again he was persuaded by Livingston that speed and surprise were the essence of success, that "Time is running out for the Royal family, as the breath of the Black Douglas is hot in their pursuit."

At that fatal conference there was another present whom I recognised. He played no part in the debating but sat still and silent while the others argued. His eyes were fixed on one man only, just as the eyes of a cat are fixed on a bird before it springs. The look in those eyes made gooseflesh start on my arms. When Sir Philip's judgement was over-ridden and the matter finally decided, this Knight quietly left the counsel room. I should have spoken to my master about him, but, ashamed of my fears, I did not disclose them. That Knight was another James Stewart, the fourth son of The Wolf of Badenoch. I had last seen him the day we escaped from Lochindorb.

We set out for Lorn, riding fast into rain, and reached Dalmally by nightfall. One of the band, John Sime, the smith's son at Duffus, was sent on ahead with letters for Queen Joan from Livingston and from Sir Philip, stressing the peaceful nature of our mission. The first sign of treachery occurred when we entered The Pass of Brander and found poor John Sime's body nailed to a birch tree. He had been stripped and shot through with arrows. Of the letters he carried there was no sign. It was possible that he had been murdered by thieves, but another, more sinister explanation crawled like a maggot in my imagination.

White torrents roared off Ben Cruachan, and the track along Loch Awe was dangerous with mud. We were ambushed on the bridge over the River Awe. They attacked out of alder and elderberry from both sides of the torrent. We had our heads down into a sting of summer hail and, too late, my war instinct shrieked, "Ambush". Once on the bridge we were trapped. We wheeled our horses back to back and prepared to fight it out. Their leader was a big man clad in black armour and mounted on a jet black horse with trappings of black leather. Sir Philip called out to him that we came in peace. I recall his words: "Sir James Stewart, Black Knight of Lorn, we wish you no harm. We come on a peaceful errand at the Queen's request."

I stared at the weird conical head of the Black Knight and wondered if such a monstrous creature could understand the King's tongue. His helmet was the ugly pointed helm the Italians had invented at the turn of the century, draped in chain mail to protect neck and shoulders. The sinister dog's snout had small breathing holes and a wide-vision slit. Unexpectedly he raised the visor and eyes, hooded by heavy brows, glared at us. There was a sudden stillness as if the scene was frozen for eternity. His words spat out flat and final.

"Hog you were, and Hog you are. Unsheath your sword, you malignant priest, and call on your evil gods to prepare your place in Hell." His visor snapped shut as he sat, still as a statue on a black stone horse. In a flash his identity came to me.

"This is not the Black Knight of Lorn but James Stewart, son of The Wolf of Badenoch." I spoke softly for Sir Philips's ears only.

"Yes, Peter." His reply was clear and heard by all. "It is James, the mysterious James." His tone was heavy. "He is no longer the boy who cursed me as he watched his mother leave Lochindorb. Hate is fed by time. He sees me as the evil genius that tore Lady Mariota from her family so many years ago. If that is what he truly believes then his hate is so deep-rooted he has only one course of action." With these last words he slowly drew his sword and spurred his charger towards his enemy.

I cannot tell you how long the battle lasted. Both men were wounded and their blood mingled with the blood of their horses on that torn and muddy road between the birch trees.

James Stewart fought like a demon. His sword rose and fell with a speed and weight I have never seen equalled. It was as if he was battering Sir Philip and his horse into the mire. Yet he was the first to be unseated. My master at that moment held his enemy's life in his hands, but he swiftly dismounted to give equal terms and the combat clashed once more. Then Sir Philip's sword described a dreadful arc to land point down through a felled tree. His severed hand clung to the hilt.

As James Stewart struck the blow that must have ended my master's life I rushed at him. I was hit by three arrows and pitched off the bridge into the River Awe. Only Percy the Fowler and I escaped. We were carried by the flooding river into Loch Etive. Somehow we made the shore and struggled to Aultchaorunm, where a family of MacDonalds cared for us and we were guided back to the Great Glen from Glencoe by that same clan.

I regret with all my heart, Lady Bridget, that I am here and your husband is not. I shall never rest till I find him and carry his body home to you.

Eighteen

On a yellow parchment, among many others in the Bishop's chest, tied by a ribbon of crumbling silk but holding the tarnished seal of the Bishop of Moray, John Winchester had added his postscript. The document was lengthy, and contained his own private and personal opinions on other matters of moment. These included his assessment of Livingston – which he begins in his testimony on the fate of Philip Hogeston – and of Crichton, and, the most dangerous comments of all, on the Black and Red Douglas. In his clear, square hand he committed to paper under his personal seal statements which could have been treasonable in the year 1440. Clearly, Bishop John had retained his position of power and influence in the years that followed only because he had had the good sense to bury his opinions in his dungeon at Spynie Palace.

This then was his "Credo". These very personal conclusions, treasonable if fate had swung the pendulum of state a fraction more to the Douglas cause, were his hostages to fortune.

"It seems certain to me," wrote the Bishop, "that Philip Hogeston and his men were duped by Livingston. Peter Grant had not heard, though he attended his master at every conference, that Queen Joan had married James Stewart of Lorn in the short time that had elapsed since her strange letter arrived in my hands. It is therefore almost certain that Sir Philip was unaware of that dramatic change of circumstance. On the other hand, it is reasonable to suppose that Livingston and his associates had this vital information before Philip arrived in Stirling. In my opinion, Livingston falsified the situation and sent Philip Hogeston on this dangerous mission deliberately misguided. Perhaps he hoped to test the defence of Lorn. But I believe there was a more subtle purpose behind the plan. The murder of a Queen's messenger by a Black Knight in the Land of Lorn would give Livingston a perfect excuse for the armed sortie against The Lord of Lorn which he had doubtless already planned and later successfully carried out. I have no doubt, however, that the scheme to impersonate Stewart of Lorn was hatched in the twisted brain of James Stewart of Badenoch.

As in all classical tragedies, including the murder of our beloved King James, memoriae bonae, the portents were there, were read, and went unheeded. Philip Hogeston's dream was clearly an unearthly warning. Lady Bridget's intuitive deduction of Queen Joan's true feelings towards the Black Knight of Lorn should have been given greater weight. Had her husband taken her advice, he would surely have suspected the duplicity of Livingston. Had he waited his son Alastair's arrival next day as he had planned, he would have been given additional information which would have changed his estimation of the Stirling faction. But he was persuaded not to wait. Peter Grant had a flash of insight concerning the silent watcher which he failed to communicate to Sir Philip for fear of looking a fool and a coward. Finally, John Sime's murder was surely an ominous warning that mischief was close at hand.

Like all classical tragedy too, the seed of disaster were already deep in the heart of the victim, implanted there by fate and by the murderer. It is plain as a pikestaff to me that, despite his nightmare premonition, Philip Hogeston under-estimated the terrible effects on young James Stewart of that appalling scene in the great hall of Lochindorb. It is clear that every fibre of James' being was, from that moment, at war with the treacherous monk. His mother, at least, understood this.

Knowing what we do, we can imagine, perhaps, what must have passed through the minds of James Stewart of Lochindorb and Philip Hogeston of Plewlands as they fought to the death at the Bridge of Awe. The Curse had come to roost."

Translator's Notes

1 The Lairdie – The death of Capt. James Brander Dunbar of Pitgaveny ended a career that is a legend now in Moray. He could have been Dr. David Rorie's "Pawky Duke". He was the original John MacNab of John Buchan's famous tale. His large estate of farms and forest included the town of Lossiemouth, the neighbouring R.A.F. station and the gloomy fortress-like place, Pitgaveny, with its scores of dusty heads of African animals. His too, was the mighty ruin of The Bishop's Palace of Spynie.

The Lairdie now awaits, no doubt with interest and impatience, his biographer.

2 The Hogeston, or Ogston family lived at Plewlands, Duffus, which in the seventeenth century became Gordonstoun. One Simon de Hogeston died there in 1240, and the family is even older than that. An Alexander Ogstoun of Plewlands was summoned to pay homage to Edward I of England, Edward Longshanks, Hammer of the Scots, at the Castle of Elgin (on Ladyhill) in 1303.

Another of the same name, six centuries later, invented an anaesthetic mask which was used the world over. Yet another introduced antiseptic surgery to the North East of Scotland, became Regius Professor of Surgery in Aberdeen from 1882 to 1909 and was made Sir Alexander Ogston in 1912.

I make this comment only to underline and explain my delight at being the one lucky enough to have literally, dug up this piece of Ogston history, on my own doorstep.

3 The Tunnel – Local tales are supported by this description of a tunnel connecting a cave near Primrose Bay with Plewlands. Gordonstoun, now the school, was built c 1500 on the foundations of the more ancient Plewlands. I have been told that, early in his school's history, Dr. Kurt Hahn caused a passage in the cellars to be bricked up to discourage "dungeoning". When I was a boy I broke through a wooden barricade into a cave near Primrose Bay similar to the one described by Philip Hogeston, and I have seen the prehistoric drawings. The cave must be known to many boys and men of the Moray coast unless it suffered the fate of "Groff Hochs". During the last war this magnificent double-legged stack of rock became the target of a demolition squad from the 8th Training Battalion of the Royal Engineers.

4 The Naked Christ – Philip Hogeston's description of this wood-carving and the comments on it by the Wolf (page 64) provided, alas, insufficient evidence for the Department of Medieval Antiquities of the British Museum to name the sculptor.

"Many figures of Christ were carved by the Italian sculptors of the thirteenth century," writes my informant, "but we cannot possibly name a sculptor without further details or, preferably, a good photograph."

The only "photograph" we have is Hogeston's vivid description of this outstanding work of art wrought by an unknown sculptor seven hundred and thirty-five years ago.

5 This poignant description of the sick boy Andrew Stewart matches exactly the appearance of a child with diphtheria. This killer took its grisly toll of life through the centuries and until recently thousands of its young victims were admitted to our fever hospitals and to our graveyards.

6 In Hogeston's day the local office of the Knights Templar was

near the North Gate of Elgin – in Lossiewynd. Later they moved to "The Tower" in High Street, where an old iron cross high on the turret of the Tower Hotel remains to remind us of this.

7 The Sixth Crusade – To the military historian this disastrous Crusade of 1396 is an example of how a brave army came near to annihilation because of incorrect intelligence and divided leadership. In brief, Bajezid the Ottoman Sultan had laid siege to Constantinople. But when he had invested the city for a year he became impatient. He withdrew a large part of his army to his Eastern borders to continue the subjugation of the Mongol tribes beyond his territories.

King Sigismund of Hungary led the Crusade and with him marched soldiers from the Balkan States and Knights from France, Scotland, England and Germany. The garrison in Rhodes sent a strong detachment.

Spies from the Easter edge of the world reported that Tamurlane, Lord of the Mongols, had bestirred himself and would soon ride with a mighty army to do battle with the Ottoman Sultan. King Sigismund's plan was to pursue the Turk and catch him as he faced the might of Tamurlane, or better still when retreating before the Mongol threat. As it happened these informants anticipated events exactly but by several years! But then no one ever knew what Tamurlane was planning. At the height of his power he ruled the world from beyond the Karakorums to the Black Sea. In his Golden City of Samarkand he held the web of his vast empire like a gigantic spider.

The Crusaders pursued Sultan Bajezid and came upon his Ottoman troops at Nicopolis in the Danube Valley. They fought well, but as nations. The Turk fought as an army, and cut them to pieces.

8 Alexander Stewart, "The Wolf of Badenoch", 1343-1405 – was the son of King Robert II of Scotland. His mother was Elizabeth Mure, the King's mistress until he married her four years after "The Wolf" was born.

Mystery surrounds the last years of Alexander Stewart's life. He died fifteen years after he had burned Elgin Cathedral and after seeking forgiveness of the Church he despised at a "Ceremony of Humiliation" in the Blackfriars Monastery, Perth. A later chronicler, Sir Thomas Dick Lauder, postulated a serious illness within these last few years. Philip Hogeston's story suggests the possible nature of such an illness. Both accounts surmise that a destructive ailment finally broke this bold and arrogant man. But nothing is certain, or ever can be now.

9 Philip Hogeston does not mention, probably because it was not to him important, that Sir Alexander Stewart, pirate, plundered a ship belonging to non other than the Lord Mayor of London, Dick Whittington.

10 At the Battle of Baugé, North of the Loire, between Tours and Angers, France was saved by the Scots. It was the turning point of the English domination. Half of France was already in their hands with the pledge of the remainder on the death of the French King. The appearance of a Scottish army in 1421 changed all that. The relief of the Castle of Dreux would have been part of the task of the force under Sir John Stewart of Darnley, whose French possessions at Evreux marched with Dreux. For his services to France, Stewart of Darnley was accorded the honour of quartering the Lilies of France on his shield.

11 The Ogstoun Cross - Where Ogstoun Market, Kirk and Cross existed in Philip Hogeston's time now stands the Michael Kirk of Gordonstoun School, the ancient Plewlands. But the Cross, which probably replaced a

Culdee or Columbian mission post, speaks its Christian message only to those with the time to listen and the ears to hear. In the days when I knew Gordonstoun best this Celtic Cross was a rallying point of the then small school founded by the late Kurt Hahn. That Cross and Duffus Castle, the caves of Covesea and the Pictish war-hills are the only links with the lives of Bridget de Dreux and Philip Hogeston which now remain North of the Loch of Spynie. By persistent drainage, the bog of Plewlands and the Lang Steps have long since become the most fertile fields in Moray. But the Loch, although greatly reduced and occupying now only the easterly one-tenth of its original extent, is still, as it always was, a paradise for wild-fowl.

12 Queen Joan – King James I of Scotland fell in love with Joan Beaufort, cousin of King Henry V of England, during his captivity at the English Court. He wrote a delightful love poem describing how, from his prison window, he saw her for the first time, walking with her ladies in the castle gardens below. By the time he met his end in his late thirties, Queen Joan had given birth seven times, and the Scottish Royal Family was enlivened by six daughters and one son, James.

It was this young family that Queen Joan sought to defend from those who contended for power, and, in particular, from the rival regents, Crichton and Livingston. Livingston snatched Joan and her children by force from her new husband, the Black Knight of Lorn, and compelled her to surrender to him her castle at Stirling, and her son James. He, the future King, had to survive some desperate and bloody adventures ere he sat firmly on the throne of Scotland.

His sisters married into European Royal Families; one Princess to the heir of Savoy, another to the Archduke of

Austria. Isobel was to wed the Duke of Brittany. Possibly the most beautiful of them all, Margaret, with the "face like starlight", was by then the Dauphine of France.

Their brother, the young James II, at the age of nineteen in Holyrood Palace, married Mary the daughter of the powerful Duke of Gueldres and niece of the Duke of Burgundy.

Thus did James I of Scotland and his Joan give strength and substance to the Auld Alliance.

To Joan Beaufort from James Stewart,
Written circa 1420

And therewith cast I doun mine eye again,
Whereas I saw, walking under the tower,
Full secretly new cummyn her to pleyne,
The fairest and the freshest younge flower
That ever I saw, methought, before that hour;
    For which sudden abate anon astert
    The blood of all my body to my hert.

And though I stood abased tho a lyte
No wonder was; for-why my wittis all
Were so owre-come with pleasure and delight,
Only through latting of mine eyen fall,
That suddenly my heart became her thrall
    For ever, of free will; for of manace
    There was no token in her sweete face.

Cover Design: The Digital Canvas Company
                  Forres
                  Scotland
                  bookcovers@digican.co.uk

Layout: Stephen M.L. Young
                  Elgin
                  Scotland
                  stephenmlyoung@aol.com

Font: Adobe Garamond (11pt)

Copies of this book can be ordered via the Internet:

                  www.librario.com

or from:

                  Librario Publishing Ltd
                  Brough House
                  Milton Brodie
                  Kinloss
                  Moray IV36 2UA
                  Tel /Fax No 01343 850 617